Vatilan the Dish Thief

Robin Llywelyn was born in 1958, in north Wales. He is Managing Director of the Italianate village of Portmeirion, created by his architect grandfather Clough-Williams Ellis, where he lives. He is the author of two novels. His first, *Seren Wen ar Gefndir Gwyn* (*White Star, Bright Sky*), won him the National Eisteddfod Prose Medal and the Arts Council of Wales Book of the Year award. It was perceived to mark a new departure in the Welsh-language novel. His second novel, another highly inventive work, *O'r Harbwr Gwag i'r Cefnfor Gwyn* (*From Empty Harbour to White Ocean*), won him the National Eisteddfod Prose Medal for a second time in 1994, and the BBC Writer of the Year award in the same year, confirming Robin Llywelyn's reputation as one of Wales's most significant contemporary authors. *Y Dŵr Mawr Llwyd*, the original Welsh text of this collection, appeared in 1995.

Vatilan the Dish Thief

Robin Llywelyn

PARTHIAN

Parthian
The Old Surgery
Napier Street
Cardigan
SA43 1ED
www.parthianbooks.co.uk

First published in Welsh as *Y Dŵr Mawr Llwyd* by Gwasg Gomer

First published in English in 2009
© Robin Llewelyn 1995
All Rights Reserved
Translated by Diarmuid Johnson © 2009

ISBN 978-1-905762-32-3

Editor: Diarmuid Johnson

Cover design by www.lucyllew.com
Inner design by books@lloydrobson.com
Typeset by books@lloydrobson.com
Printed and bound by Lightning Source

Translated with the support of Welsh Literature Exchange
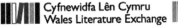
Cyfnewidfa Lên Cymru
Wales Literature Exchange

Published with the financial support of the Welsh Books Council
CYNGOR LLYFRAU CYMRU
WELSH BOOKS COUNCIL

British Library Cataloguing in Publication Data

A cataloguing record for this book is available from the British Library

Contents

The Sea is Very Full

'Why did you have to chuck all my things into the sea?' you said. It was a bright moonlit night, and your eyes gleamed in the light of the open window. Dawn seemed close: the bleating of sheep reached us from the upper shore.

I had seen you speak like this in your sleep before, eyes open like this as you slept. And now I stared into your eyes and whispered, 'There now, my love,' I said, 'sleep now.'

'What about my things?' you said.

'What things do you mean?' I said. I couldn't tell whether you were sleeping or whether you were awake.

'All my things,' you said, still staring past me into the eye of the moon. A young dawn was beginning to climb the bedroom walls. 'My wellingtons, my jacket, and my sandwiches: you flung them all right out to sea.' Your voice seemed distant. 'It was your idea to go to the beach,' you reproached then. 'We were in the middle of these big sand-dunes, we were going to have tea on the beach. I was barefoot. I put my jacket in one wellington, and my sandwiches in the other. And then you got up, and grabbed my things, and flung them right out to sea. You thought it was a funny thing to do, I suppose. You had a good laugh, that's for sure, and you tried to get me to fetch them from the water.'

'Why did you have to keep your sandwiches in your sea-boots?' I said, imagining this a strange place to keep one's food. I tried to remember when we had last had a trip to the beach.

'They were wrapped in wax-paper, weren't they. You're the one who wanted to picnic. And I had put a couple of sandwiches together, and wrapped them up in a nice little pack. The food was for me, it was for both of us, and then you flung the whole lot out to sea. There was no food for us to share after that.'

'And what did you do then?'

'Well, I went to fish my things out of the water, didn't I? What else could I do? But a great big wave came to meet me, and then all the other waves broke over my head. I managed to jump clear of the great big one, or I would have drowned there and then. But the waves were swelling around me, carrying me away from you, and I could see they were driving past me toward the beach to break on the sand-dunes where we had been sitting, and the shoreline was receding, and I couldn't make it back to you. I just watched you on the dune-tops, one hand shielding your eyes. And I heard you laugh as you turned your back. You hurried back to the upper shore, your feet nice and dry, with nothing to hold you back, while my feet shot to the depths of the sea.'

'Did you manage to escape the sea in the end, in your dream?'

'Yes, it seems I did. Otherwise I wouldn't be here, would I? And no thanks to you either. I don't know how I got back. The current was sweeping me out into the ocean and I was helpless to fight it. I saw the cliffs at Craig Ddu, and the rocks tearing the water with their teeth, and dark splotches of seaweed in the foam, and the moon, yellow and motionless. And I felt the pull take hold of me, and I was so tired, and I felt an urge to let myself slip into the arms of the seaweed and be made love to by the strong waters. My resistance was broken. I was overcome by the struggle. I wanted peace, nothing more. I could feel the blood-warm water around me. How lovely to slip under its silken sheets. To watch the bubbles rise as I sank. How lovely to relax one's grip and just let go. Until I found the bottom rising to meet me, the shells on the seaweed-covered rocks hurting my toes. That's when I raised my head and broke the surface and there I was trying to make out the pathway climbing from the cliff edge. I thought I saw it, but there was no sign of the sea-boots nor the coat nor the sandwiches nor anything else. And you were gone too.'

'You must have been steaming mad at me?'

I was looking out of the open window at the path of the moon which was still shining weakly on the great grey expanse of the sea.

'At you?' Your voice was without emotion. 'There was nothing left in me to stir up. And you couldn't have cared less, could you? I could see that. You had flung all my things into the sea and laughed as you turned away. I was annoyed with you. I was annoyed with myself for having once believed the things you said.... Annoyed that I had to walk barefoot across sharp rocks. Annoyed that I had to traipse around

3

looking for you again. Do you know why I had to look for you? So that I could tell you. I walked the streets of the seaside resorts asking after you. I wandered past the plastic bucket and yellow spade shops, past the soap bubbles and the seasonal English, across the harbour bridge to the quayside, asking all I knew whether they had seen you around, but no one wanted to help. It was music to their ears. All the tongues I set wagging, going round barefoot, my head covered with sand and my hair hanging over my face.

All I remember then is night falling while I continued to search for you. Then I arrived back here, and it must have been late because there you were snoring merrily deep in your bed, refusing to wake when I wanted to ask "Why?" But you've woken up at last, haven't you, my little angel? So now I can ask you: why did you go and fling all my things into the sea?'

I remember trying to explain that I was really sorry, that it was a terrible thing to do, of course, but that after all it was only a dream and nothing had really happened. I'd never have done such a thing, even in a dream. 'I would never have thrown all your things into the sea,' I said.

'But you did,' you replied.

'Ah, come on now,' I said. 'It's almost sunrise. Dreaming belongs to the night. It's high time for you to forget this nonsense about throwing all your things into the sea.' Perhaps my voice was just a shade tetchy. I had only just woken up, my head was heavy and I badly needed a good cup of coffee. I left the bedroom now thinking I'd make us a cup each and show you once and for all that everything was alright. I went to fetch your sea-boots from the cupboard under the stairs, and your jacket from the wardrobe so you could see I was telling the truth.

4

But when I looked under the stairs your sea-boots weren't there, and nowhere in the wardrobe was your jacket to be seen. You were still lying on the bed staring straight ahead of you. I put the tray on the bedside table with the breakfast things on it. Your face seemed so pale I thought, your lips so still. I leaned over to kiss you on the lips. They were cold. Only when I raised my head to take a proper look at you did I realise that your hair was full of tiny grains of sand that glistened like the stars.

Morris Wind and Ifan Rain

Morris Wind is in the doorway asking whether he may come in. He presses his face to the window and scrapes at the glass with his nails. The world is too big, the task overwhelming. He wants to rest in a nice, cosy place. He won't disturb her, he promises to behave, he won't wreck the pictures or knock the tables over. It's just that she thinks he is big; she must remember that the bigger something seems at a distance, the smaller it will be once held in the hand. Not he that blasted the woods last night and stole the leaves. Good Lord, no! Not he that stirred the sea up and had it thrashing over the fences right onto the houses. And he never prises his fingers under the eaves to raise the roofs like the lid of a box. It's all the fault of the restless spirit of Gwyn ap Nudd and his clan. It's the fault of Bendigeidfran. They all want to ride the skies on his back. They swarm around him, straddle him, thrust their pointed stirrups into his sides and whip him mercilessly with their rods of fire. Who can blame him for wailing and groaning when subjected to their thuggery? He's trying to dislodge them, that's all. Has to drop everything and run like a fox from the hounds. Such a shame they won't leave him in peace to see to his duties. Turning windmills to grind the grain into food for little children is work for the wind. Filling bright sails and speeding them over the ocean wave is too. Carrying cuckoos as they migrate from Africa is another of his tasks, but he has little time to make a fist of it. These are the simple things which give him pleasure, not mischief-making, but they refuse to leave him be and sometimes he just loses his mind. He's been on the run for quite some time, he's fled from one end of the globe to the other, but the restless spirits are ever on his heels, goading and tormenting him. And now he's just given them the slip for five minutes, shaken them off for the first time in ages, please won't she open the door? Or the window... just so he can come in, just for a short time, and if he may, may Ifan Rain follow him in too? Ifan is here, crying to be let into the house.

No, you may not come in, you pulled the place asunder last time. I was silly enough to believe your nonsense, Morris, and gullible enough to think that old Ifan's tears were for real. You're a bad lot. Tell Ifan to go home to his nest in the north where the rain falls like eggs from a well, we don't want his type around here. Tell him to go the heart of the African desert where the sun is hot and the throats of snakes tighten with thirst, he'll be welcome there. He's not needed here, and neither are you, Morris. Get the hell out of here, you caused enough trouble last time you called late.

But Ifan is very sorry for what he did, Mrs my dear, we won't do it again. He's crying to come in, really he is Mrs,

7

can't you here him plead? We're not leaving here until we're allowed in. We've come a long way to see you, Mrs, we thought surely we'd be made welcome. Has our welcome grown cold here, Mrs? Surely you can't be angry at us for last time? She's happy to see us under it all, Ifan, she'll come to her senses in a minute don't you worry and then we'll be allowed into the house. C'mon Ifan, get up on my back, we'll go for a little run over hill and dale in the bosom of the eastern sky and give dear Mrs a chance to rustle us up a good feed.

But you said we'd be able to make ourselves at home here. What should we do now then, Morris? I'm tired travelling the boundless bright starry miles on your back. I don't want to go for a little run with you. I'm soaked to the skin, and these rags I'm wearing are worthless when the cold claws me to the marrow. Gorgeous rags though. They're no protection from that great hail that belts in from the mountain. I'm scared of it, Morris, and it'll come looking for me tonight and batter me black and blue and dump me into the sea. I can't take another night like that. So please ask her again, Morris, ask her to let us into the house. You and Mrs dear are all pally wally, that's what you said, you really get on, best friends. I can't believe you'd lead me astray like this. Tell her again we won't make a mess, since you two are so close. Tell her we were just a bit clumsy last time, clumsy and careless, I was young rain then, all legs like a colt, knives and forks were new to me – and remember to tell her I'm sorry about the dishes. Remember to tell her it was you who turned the tables over and smashed the pictures and blew the fire up the chimney, not Ifan Rain. *You* made the partition shake, not me. You tell her I'll come in on my own. I did very little to offend last time. Listen, if I should be let in, I'll put in a good word for you, and maybe she'll come to her senses then and let you in too. And if she refuses to listen, I'll sneak in through the back door when she turns her back and let you in anyway, and she'll see then that we're not really such a terribly bad wind and rain.

May Ifan come into the house on his own then, Mrs dear? He promises to behave, it wasn't his fault last time, was it? I understand you won't be wanting me, of course I do, but why punish poor Ifan as he's not done anything wrong? Come on, Mrs dear, open the door an inch or two, he promises to behave.

You keep your distance then, Morris Wind, off with you to the beach where I can see you churning up the waves. Now then, Ifan Rain, and only if you promise to be good, come in for a minute, but none of your horse-play, or you'll be out on your ear, do you understand? Heavens, you're dripping wet my lad! Take yourself to the back this minute and take off those wet rags before you catch your death. You'll find plenty of clean towels in the hot press. There are some of my son's old clothes in the chest – they'll do you fine for now. Come on now, give me those old things so I can dry them in front of the fire. You're shaking like a leaf, lad. Are you sure your not ill? Here, you should take a nice warming cuppa, and a piece of toast, and you'll soon feel better, you'll be right as rain.

You're really kind to me, Mrs dear, thanks so much. This toast is really good. I'll keep a little piece for Morris for when I have to go back out to him later. Poor devil, left to shiver outside in the cold, and hide from the restless spirits. They pester him mercilessly you know, that's what drives him out of his mind, that's what makes him do bad things. Of course, he's better off now than he used to be – Gwyn has kept some of the spirits back to help him with family affairs, so Morris manages to get away more often because there are fewer of them to catch him sometimes. If he were allowed into the house, you'd see how much he's changed already. It's 'please and thank you' every time now, he's a real gentleman is our Morris Wind these days. But there we are, it seems he must be punished. Of course, he's suffered for what he did – a bad conscience his every waking minute – o yes, even a buffeting old wind like Morris has his conscience. He's suffered his darts of remorse, showers of them, all on top of the flaming spurs the restless spirits tire his butt with. No wonder the poor guy gets all worked up and spins around wildly on the spot like a dog with a sore ass; trees, houses, sea and ships all spinning wildly with him, rising like smoke into the sky, and wherever he goes he leaves his footprint like a furrow across the land. But he won't do it again, he's promised not to, if he's allowed into the house.

Well call him in then, for goodness sake. But remember Ifan, I hold you responsible for his behaviour. Any horseplay and you'll both be out. Do you both like fried potatoes? They'll be on the table when you get back.

Morris, where are you ? She says you can come in... I said a gap would open up... Morris! Morris Wind! Shelter for the night at long last, and now he's disappeared! Where the hell is he? I'd be better off without him, God knows. Everything's gone so quiet, not a stir in the treetops, nothing but a hint of foam on top of the waves. Hey you, sea-breeze, have you seen Morris Wind anywhere? He was over on the bay just a minute ago, stirring up the waters hellishly, but look now, everywhere is so still. Did you see him on the horizon a few minutes ago? Over there where the shafts of sunlight are casting patterns on the water? O, now I see. He's gone a long way! Are the restless spirits still on his back? Bring him a message from me, will you? For whom? What do you mean? You should know, I'm Ifan Rain. I'm one of the greater elements, you know, master of lesser puffs of halfling winds like you. So off with you now, and tell him Ifan Rain says he's to come to the house. Come on, be a good breeze, chop chop.

I'm beginning to worry, Mrs dear. He should have arrived by now. Mm, the fried spuds were great. Shh, did you hear scratching at the window? It must be Morris come back. I wonder what kept him? Gosh, he must be completely exhausted. Look at him all in a huddle on the doorstep. Come on in, Morris my friend, come in and warm yourself at the fire. Morris, Mrs dear has fried you some potatoes. Here, put your arm round my shoulder.... Look Mrs dear, see the state he's in, he looks like he's been halfway round the world. Look Mrs dear, he's like a suckling lamb. He's completely out of breath. Do you believe me now, Mrs dear? He'll cause no trouble tonight.

Well yes, you seem a lot more subdued than when you were last here pulling the place apart and throwing your weight about. You seem more mature, as elements go. You may come whenever you like, you're most welcome, I'll be glad of your company. My son left home long ago, and since his dad passed away, bless him... but come along, Morris. Change out of those filthy rags or we'll never get you warm. Ifan will show you where. And here, here's a pair of slippers each for you. Of course, you won't be going home tonight, I'll make up two beds for you in the back room in no time...

you'll feel much better for a good night's sleep.

Ifan, do you feel alright? I'm itching all over and my skin seems too small for my body. I can't get used to her son's clothes. I want my magic rags back so I can swell up and grow. Get out of bed and help me search for them. They must be on the line or on the clothes-horse by the fire. Come on, hurry, we better get up, work is calling. You go down stairs to look for the rags Ifan, so we can swell up and up and be bad as bad can be. It's a shame really that we should have to wreck the house now, we were made so welcome. Does it worry you sometimes, Ifan, you know, having to wreck people's houses and everything? Yeah, it comes with the job, I know, but... anyway, hurry up and get our clothes back, will you, it was your doing, clean clothes and all that....

Did you both sleep well, Ifan? Forget about those old rags for a minute. Most important of all, is Morris feeling better after his little sleep? Much better. The poor fellow has had a rough time of late, hasn't he? The bacon and eggs will be ready in a jiffy... what now? Yes, those rags you were wearing when you got here, what of them? What do you mean your work clothes? Those clothes weren't fit for a clown in the circus, lad. They were completely soaked and stank like a polecat, I wouldn't call them clothes at all. Well, I can't give them to you, Ifan. I've burnt them. I threw them on the fire last night after you had gone to bed. You can keep the clothes I gave you. My son won't be needing them again. You won't have to wander the world-over like tramps. What's wrong, Ifan? You look like you've seen a ghost. Sit down over here, good lad, here's a glass of water. You poor hand is shaking, Ifan. What's wrong, Ifan?

Where are the rags, Ifan? Why haven't you brought them

back? We have to put them back on. What's the matter, Ifan? Have you seen a ghost or something? Where are the magic bloody rags, Ifan? I want to know, where the hell are they? We can't wreck the house or flood the land without the magic rags, Ifan, so where are they? Are they in the warm cupboard or hanging out on the line or what? Hurry up, will you, I want to put them on and fill the air up and get up to my nasty old tricks. I want to be wild and windy again and I don't give a damn about the restless spirits either! Now where are my clothes please, Ifan?

Often, on a Sunday afternoon, Morris Wind and Ifan Rain may be seen walking the dyke along the beach. During the week, they tend to help Mrs dear with the house work: hoovering, washing dishes, running errands. When the weather is fine, they sometimes do a spot of gardening, growing vegetables – potatoes, carrots and the like. Every Wednesday, after lunch, they take the Little Bus to market, but they never buy anything. They wander around the marketplace, have a cuppa in one of the cafés, and home in time for tea. But on Sunday afternoon, they walk the dyke. They walk slowly, watching the seagulls circle the castle. They stop to watch the boat-like sun sink into the bay. Things seem larger somehow, and the world has become strange. They find themselves needing to rest on a bench to draw breath. On the path at the foot of the bench is a white shell left there by a child or seagull. They hold it to their ear each in turn to hear the sea's great roar within. The sea's voice says: the greater things seem at a distance, the lesser when you hold them in your hand.

A Contribution to the Biography of the Right Reverend Brother Stotig Isgis

For some time now, it has been my intention to publish the biography of one of the most remarkable saints of our time. Long years of research and endless digging stand between me and accomplishing that task, but let the present pages serve to whet the appetite of any diligent scholars who may wish to graze the lush pastures of the lives of our sacred heroes.

For much of his life, the right reverend Brother Stotig Isgis was a serf in the parish of Eithin in the Diffwys region. Seen from without, there is nothing to suggest that his life be in the least remarkable. Until the time of his military service, he lived the life of a common serf. Rising at dawn, venturing out whatever the weather to plunder the neighbours, drink himself senseless in the tavern by night, and home in time to batter his mother. However, during the six years of his military service, Isgis was utterly transformed from hairy-handed serf into merciless thief and hellish doer of ill. His name was rape, pillage and vengeance and grew to instil terror into the hearts of young children throughout the land. Following his successful career in the army, he sought to become a monk, was duly ordained, and lived for the rest of his days – yet to end – humbly and meekly, his heart, more often than not, interceding on behalf of others, rather than on behalf of his own good self.

Such a bare picture from birth until death (yet to be). There is little to say of the public figure, and as for the inner man, to search the dark recesses of the soul would surely be a painful affair in the eyes of God. Wouldn't it be a blasphemous thing to lay bare the soul of a Christian? Despite all this, and in the reassuring belief that nothing in the world can dent the sanctity of our reverend, pious Stotig, he who came into the world unsound of mind, and shall leave it just so, I will seek to part retrace his life and times, in the hope of shedding a glimmer of the saint's ardent light on all who read my words.

In the war of the Lamb, the heart is the field of battle. And the heart is deep. In the heart's depths, the life of the true Christian resides. And those who venture into the secret haunts of this green glade come face to face with the mysteries of life itself. Those who have endeavoured with pure heart to dwell on inner states of being will know how arduous, how impossible it is to arrive at complete understanding, even for a fleeting moment, of the covert ways of the soul, because, in its intensity, the heart touches on that place which knows neither path nor boundary.

Brother Stotig did not understand this. In fact, he understood very little. But he knew much in his instinctive heart of hearts. He knew, for example, how to sneak past everyone into the refectory at dinner time. In fact, this was the beginning of my doings with him, in the early and innocent days of my budding monastic career. I asked him to verse me in the art of ghosting in ahead of the rest. I remember his care and patience as he taught me. How carefully he showed me how to prepare smoke-bombs and then drop them from a height onto the company while shouting 'Fire! Fire!' Fond memories of his grabbing my hand and our rushing together through the doors for the best seats, our monks' habits floating after us. Yes, Brother Stotig was a cunning monk. Day in day out I marvelled at his ability to confound the Brothers Zebra and lay the blame at the door of other Brothers who knew less of the taste of success. My admiration for him was unfailing, I sought to model myself on him, he was my teacher.

Indeed, in my enthusiasm to learn as much as I could from him, I recorded very little of what he ever told me. And now, as I gather my notes together, it's a source of great surprise and deception to me to see that all that remains is one postcard and two invoices for washing his dirty socks. Is this the only evidence that survives of our relationship? No, because in the vaults of memory there endure a great many recollections of him, of his anecdotes and doings. More than anything else, these are the foundation of this biography. And the first of them is the story of his time of birth and of the years of his tender childhood.

As was the wont of many serfs at the time, his father, Ulbig Isgis, always had a warm welcome for pilgrims and alms-seekers of no fixed abode. On holy days, the house would be heaving, and, on the morrow of the feast, the guests would invariably relieve the household of all its belongings, leaving after them not as much as a handkerchief. Once, about Easter time, when he was two years old, Stotig lifted his head in the cradle and asked his mother: 'why do all these good strange people make off with our belongings every time they call?' His mother was unable to enlighten him, because she herself didn't know the answer. The determined lad asked his father the same question when, later that evening, the latter was spilled out of a wheelbarrow.

Ulbig went over to the little child, lifted him into his arms – such was his awe that he was now sober as a judge – and cried out in wonder: 'Hear that! With a tongue as sharp as that, the lad will go far!' And with that remark, he gave the boy a push through the open door headlong into the dung heap next to the house. 'And maybe that'll teach you not to stick your nose where it's not needed!' This experience exercised considerable influence on the young Stotig.

Stotig Isgis' childhood was disastrous rather than unhappy. As he grew older, he came to realise how disadvantageous it was to be son of a filthy, uncouth serf, and he fled into the woods. He made an attempt to have a family of black bears adopt him, but they turned him down. He returned to his family, his tail between his legs, and decided to make the best of a bad situation. A young, handsome and able-bodied youth, rest assured that he was not unpopular in the village. He could count as friends each and every one of the local lads, enjoyed walking out with the parish maids, drinking spirits and yellow beer, dancing and playing the fiddle, thieving and murdering with abandon; in short, he was no different to any other of the young parish blades. The lovely red-headed, blue-eyed maids of the church of Saint Elibwbana in the parish of Lower Eithin were all eyes on Sundays when looking on him.

As for him, he was drawn by their charms, drawn to one more than to any other, and before marriage was evoked, one balmy summer's evening, in the hedgerow at the head of Cae Pen Stanc, they did as often young and derisive couples do.

Next morning, as they worked together, his father asked him: 'where were you last night, my son? My heart was sorely anxious for you.' 'Having it off with Swllt y Sgwd in Ydfab Pen Stanc's ditch, if you must know, my father. I hear you'd been there before me. Has Mam heard?'

I didn't hear the rest of the tale from Brother Stotig, nor has it been recorded, and more's the pity, because it tells us much about the inner conflict the monk-to-be endured during this trying period of his life before embarking on an alternative career. In the hope of gaining further insight, I visited the Saint's native village where I met his father who by then had reached the ripe old age of one hundred and ten. When he realised who I was, he came out and welcomed me with open arms. I managed to evade his clutch, but when I enquired pointedly about the event described above, his welcome cooled considerably, and I was imprisoned for a time in the drainage system of the family lavatory at the bottom of the garden.

Another important event in the holy young man's development took place one sobering January morning when snow enveloped the hovel. The family was woken by a scratching noise by the kitchen door. 'Go out and stamp on those damn thieving birds,' shouted Ulbig from his bed. Mrs Isgis opened the door, and who should she see stretched out on the ground but Sglaffen Cook. Once thawed on the stove, a measure of turnip spirits poured through a funnel down his gullet, a hot cake shoved into his cheek, Sglaffen was revived and came to his senses.

'You've been away,' said Stotig's mother.

'Yes, Amlen Isgis, I've been away from home,' said Sglaffen.

'For quite a time,' said Stotig's mother.

'The interval was considerable,' said Sglaffen.

'How was the weather on your holidays?' asked Stotig Isgis.

'I wasn't on holiday, you daft child, I was on pilgrimage in distant climes. A pilgrimage to the tomb of a martyr of the Faith who stood up for us when the tempest consumed him, who stood up for us when the ocean drenched him, who stood up for us when the world was closing in on him. A pilgrimage to the resting place of the ashes of Saint Chwithgoch, the greatest and foremost of all saints, and my own personal favourite.' Tears glistened in the corners of the old woman's eyes. 'He was a saintly man, a good man, without a shadow of a doubt.'

Stotig was gob-smacked by her words. If this fellow was a good and saintly man, this means God is here with us, so I needn't go in search of him, because he's here in this room now, and everywhere else, he thought astutely to himself. From then on, in the knowledge that he had found faith, the young man underwent great change. The life of the monk began to beckon, but this monk had ideas of his own. And so he wrote to several orders: The White Brothers, The Black Brothers, The Zebra Brothers.

When some time had passed, he asked his father's permission to doff his layman's attire. 'What's got into you, you wretch?' said the father. 'No son of mine will ever walk the street ass-bare to the world.' Stotig explained his wish to wear the monk's habit. 'You have enough bad habits as it is,' came the reply. But little by little, Ulbig came to see that his son's intentions to become a monk were earnest, and he soon realised that the family would be a damn sight better off to see the back of this young cuckoo who devoured the food of three men and could knock back a tavernful of booze, but never contributed a flea to his upkeep, preferring to snort in bed until midday and then call for his breakfast.

'My son,' said Ulbig one evening as the two vied for position by the stove. 'I've considered long and hard your request for permission to be ordained in the orders of religion, and I find myself in concord and in agreement with you. Alas, the sleepless nights I have spent tossing and turning this harrowing decision in my mind! Bless you my son, you may go to sea on Hugh Pugh's... no, that was your brother... o, yeah: you may become a monk straight away and live like a crab without a woman, you may leave immediately without further ado, you weird little sod! But, of course, first of all you must do your military service.'

'Yes, yes, yes!' shouted Stotig, because, given the delicate state he was in, he was open to any offers made him. He was made acquainted with the idea that he must first fight before becoming a monk. He was happy to join the army. He became versed in the arts of weaponry and killing. To his knowledge, he was a monk, and even his commander didn't have the heart to tell him that soldier he was and monk he was not. Until his last breath – yet to be drawn – his wont was a gun by his side and a clutch of bombs at hand. 'My work in this world, here where we find ourselves, is to kill plenty of the faithless.' This saying crossed his lips not infrequently. 'And kill them I will, dirty pagans.'

His father's influence on our saint has been acknowledged by all, save a handful of self-styled 'scholars'. Their brains are small as an ant's egg split in two (the egg, not the ant), and so their claims are incorrect. Years after I had come to know and love him as a father, once in the middle of dinner, he honoured me with one of his rare yet oh so precious confessions. A tear or two ran from his eyes and his lip shook three times. 'I never filled my father's stockings,' he said. 'Actually, he was buried in his stocking feet. He was a very illiterate man. He never quite managed to learn the Lord's Prayer. His own particular version springs to mind: "Our Father, it's hard in heaven, hello what's his name. Thai prawns well done, I'm still half-dead with thirst...." More quick tears filled the old saint's eye as he remembered his father's prayer. 'My father thought he was a saint,' he said. He lifted his pious face to the window and stared out into the distance. 'Poor innocent man.' He dried his eyes on his sleeve. 'My father had another quote from the Bible,' he said distantly. "The lard with some pepper, I shall not want." My poor father, he knew next to nothing. He thought Noah's flood happened on a Friday, and that that was why we ate fish on that day. His only way of telling the Son of God from Father Christmas was the way they dressed. He was an utterly ignorant, deceitful and filthy man. I learned everything I know from him.'

Ulbig Isgis had a very large family. Father, mother, nine sons and eighteen daughters, all living merrily under one roof. How I cherish the story told to me by the Reverend Brother, when, in his ninety eighth year, he told of the little close-knit family sitting by the fire telling their tales all night, and drawing straws for the privilege of sleeping on the bed. The older lads worked the croft with their father. One bitter Friday in January, as they harvested near Gwaun Galed, it fell to the future monk to make the midday meal. Forgetting it was Friday, he prepared a side of pig roasted on a spit over live charcoal. All ate of the pig, but Stotig Isgis' father kept a piece in his purse unknown to any. Forty years later, when on his death bed, Stotig Isgis' father turned to him. 'My son,' he said, 'do you remember that Friday when we harvested Gwaun Galed, and you gave us pork to eat. It tasted like flesh from the cemetery to me. Here's a piece I kept from that day until this. Taste it! Isn't it disgusting?'

'Well, father,' said Stotig, spitting the foul meat to the floor, 'food *will* go off over a period of forty years. You should have complained at the time instead of keeping it to your heart like this. If you had mentioned it at the time, I could have offered you a boiled egg or something, but, you know, forty years on, what can I do but say sorry. You did eat it all at the time, if I remember correctly.'

'I didn't want to hurt you, my boy. I knew how sensitive you were about your cooking. But tell me this, my son, why did you choose to give us pork?'

'Because the lamb looked none too healthy, father. The lambs had died of some infection, and while cheap, the green meat didn't really appeal to me.'

'But, my son,' the father interjected, trying to pull himself up onto his wizened elbow, 'it was Friday.'

'Was it?' Stotig scratched his chin. 'Well, my father, maybe I forgot what day it was.'

'But how could you have forgotten something like that?'

'Maybe, my father, in the same way you forgot that it was

January, seven months before harvest time. Maybe, dear father, the way you forgot to sow the seed that year and every year both before and after? Maybe, my father, in the same way that you forgot to wash any part of your body from the day you were born? These things happen to a man sometimes, father, and I really am sorry if the pork wasn't to your taste....' To my great tribulation, I have no record of the outcome of this interesting dialogue in which are revealed to us a good number of our saint's virtues.

The pious youth was ever busy with village life. Song, dance and courting were his delight. On fair day, and holidays, he could be seen with his fiddle, entertaining the people and raising spirits. Late one John's Eve fair, Stotig and his good friend Lyshog Pen Llau were seen setting out for town. Stotig's fiddle and Lyshog's pipe were full of the wild music of the heath as they and their dark shadows filled the streets, striding resolutely to... to meet the cobbler's sons and a number of their supporters. The eldest, a big sinewy boor named Crafwr, came to meet them first. He grasped Stotig's fiddle, spat in the saint's face, and scrunched the instrument underfoot. A small group of local girls had gathered around them. Someone coughed in the silence. Here, in Stotig's words, is what happened next:

'I decided to give in to the burly lad, and bowed my head low towards the ground. But I became ashamed to show my lack of courage in front of the girls. I remembered having explained to a number of them how brave I was when it came to fighting. I could hear the cobbler's son goading me, and, eyes down, could see the large rocks about my feet. Head still bowed, I explained dispassionately to Crafwr the Cobbler's son that it was wrong of him to have destroyed my fiddle. I heard him laugh dryly as, clutching a heavy stone, I stood upright and planted it in the middle of his face. He stood like a tree in a storm for a moment, and then fell to the ground. I only just avoided the blood which spouted from his mouth. Unfortunately, a drop or two did catch one of my shoes, and I got a telling off from Mother for making a mess. But I had no further trouble with Crafwr, because he died. I sincerely believe that this is when I came to realise that playing fiddle and pipes can lead to bereavement, and so decided to dedicate the rest of my life to the service of God.'

Here we see the young monk in the thick of youth's hue and cry being summoned, perhaps for the first time, to present himself at the gates of a life of spiritual achievement, a life destined for him since the hour of his birth. I condemn those authors who, when treating of our dear monk, his life and work, sometimes suggest brazenly that our hero received no little encouragement along the path preordained for him by the fact that joining an ecclesiastical order, especially that of the Zebra Brothers, brought with it sanctuary even for a murderer. These good and upright authors fail to understand that, at the time in question, everyone in these parts was murdering the other, and that Stotig Isgis is no exception to the rule. It was a completely natural thing for him to join the Zebra Brothers.

Stotig served his military service with the royal battalion of the Rural Serfs in their camp near the city of Cracyr. On Saint Bivis' Eve, he started out with two of his fellow soldiers to seek amusement in town. They came to one of the large, radiant, beauteous wine bars on the main square where there was song, dance and celebration under the crystal lights. They were shown to a white-napped table, then ordered food and drink before concentrating their efforts, as the occasion required, on lively conversation and leg-pulling. But Stotig contributed not as much as a word to the proceedings. Soon his good friend Rachabovlav turned to him and asked: 'What's up, Stotig, someone stole your pudding, or your dessert? Tell us who's stolen your pudding and we'll give him a choking!'

'No one has stolen my pudding, because I ordered none,' replied the young soldier, a distant look in his eyes. 'The first two courses were sufficient.'

'What's on your mind then, Stotig, presuming you have one?'

'I was thinking,' said Stotig, 'thinking about us here in this tavern, drinking and eating the best of food and tasting pure vodka in crystal glasses while sweet music plays in the void and we flirt with the girls and kiss them as we please... and yet, and this very time, on top of Moel Anial in the middle of the snow, wind cutting through them like glass, the barefoot, destitute monks are making their way under the weight of penitence to the midnight mass, not having slept these past four months. And I wondered, who is better off tonight – we, at the height of our mirth, or they, poor monks, in the middle of the cold and cruel snows?'

'Make no mistake,' said Rachabovlav, drinking deeply of his vodka. 'The monks have it better tonight, no doubt about it.'

'If that be true,' said Stotig in astonishment – it is said that light like sunlight shot from his eyes – 'if what you say is true, I wish to become a monk, because I would think it difficult to be better off than we are here, and if the monks are better off than us, their lives must indeed be wonderful, and it sounds like the very thing for me.'

'Your man would believe the tallest of tales,' whispered Rachabovlav in Postyn Byddar's ear. 'Don't try and convince him of the truth, or he'll be sorely let down.'

'What?' said the deaf Postyn Byddar.

'Nothing,' said Rachabovlav.

'What?' said Postyn Byddar.

'Shut it, stupid,' said Rachabovlav, shoving his good friend off his stool who rolled out onto the floor causing the dancers to trip over him.

Next morning, Stotig Isgis removed his soldier's uniform and ran onto the street shouting: 'I'm a monk, I'm a monk'. He has taken in a sack to the Zebra Brothers, to the abbot of Moel Anial monastery.

'My son,' said the Abbot Badach to him, 'today you are naked as the very day you came into this world. Come here, my son, so that I may smear your body with holy oil.'

'Keep your old paws to yourself!'

'No need to kick or bite, son.'

'I'm no son of yours, you old fart,' shouted Stotig. 'Who the hell do you think you are?' Stotig dealt the old man a cruel swipe on the snout and blood rushed from his nose.

'Poor innocent child, I am the Abbot Badach. And you shouldn't have done that. For you are the Brother Stotig who in years to come will be renowned for having spent years in a hole underground with nought to eat or drink but barley bread and dishwater, hearing never a word all that time save his own prayers and an occasional "May I come out now, please?"

'What are you on about, you thick mule. I have no intention of spending years in a hole...'

'Wrong,' said the Abbot, finger and thumb fast on his nose

to stem the blood.

He turned to his henchmen, Malwr and Gwasgwr. 'Take him away,' he said, and snapped his fingers. 'See you in twenty years, Stotig, all being well, that is.' He whispered another word or two in his disciple's ear, and then struck him viciously with a knotted knuckle.

'No, no, Abbot Badach,' said the wretched serf, bawling his eyes out as he was dragged away. 'Abbot Badach, I am without toothbrush, please let me go, at least let me pull on my pyjamas... I'll perish in the dark.' His wild interjections echoed through the stone corridors as the sound of footsteps slowly faded. In the calm of the night, an iron door was heard closing with an iron clang, and then silence returned. Abbot Badach reached for a cream cake from the silver dish by his elbow, and greedily sunk his false teeth in it. What a sweet cake, he thought to himself.

Some years later, when the reverend brother had long become accustomed to his sub-terrestrial home, I visited him on Christmas morning and learned from him a most breathtaking piece of news. Voice quavering, he said: 'The lost art of the Zebra Monks.' With blackened, long-nailed finger, he pointed to a hole in his troglodyte wall. 'A discovery of great importance,' he added. 'A medieval mural. You must tell Badach.'

When I was lifted out of the dank hole, I immediately went to see the Abbot Badach. I told him all I had heard. He became most agitated, and a strange look filled his eyes. 'Are you very fond of cream cakes?' he asked cautiously.

In no time at all, Brother Stotig had been lifted from his horrid den. He was bathed in a bath of marble, clothed in habit and chasuble, and brought before a press conference.

This is a report on the discovery as it appeared in *The Parochial Serf*:

> '... *the mural was found by the Reverend Brother Stotig Isgis as he scraped earth and stones from a tunnel he was digging under the monastery. At a press conference, the Rev. Isgis said: 'I was extremely happy in the hole, honestly. Twenty years, that's not so much, is it? God was with me down there until about two years ago, but we had a misunderstanding and he left. I'd like to emphasise that I was not trying to escape from the hole.'*
>
> *We understand that, given the delicate nature of the mural, it will not be on view for some time. It seems that Rev. Isgis is the only person to have seen it to date. 'This is utterly thrilling', said the monastery spokesperson for unlikely matters. 'Our Brother Stotig has described an extraordinary scene. It seems that nothing like this picture has ever been seen under the sun. The Abbot has ordered current bread and scones for tea, and in this way will celebrate the discovery.'*

After the celebrations, I had the privilege of being the first to see the mural. I was lead by the Reverend Stotig himself. His voice trembled with emotion as he explained to me: 'This is the most important discovery I have ever made. It was as if day had dawned on me.' I was lead through the cells' iron gates, and down a flight of narrow stone steps into the depths of the earth. At the bottom there hung a rope ladder, and we went down the ladder into the dungeon. After a long descent, we came to the mouth of a tunnel, pushed our way into it, and crawled at full stretch, faces hardly an inch from the ground. Right at the bottom, with the help of the flash-lamp, I could see a large smooth slab displaying a number of stratchings not unlike a primitive attempt at a game of OXO.

'There you are,' said Stotig behind me.

'That's all?'

'See how the circles represent the Almighty, and the crosses are an early attempt to analyse the sacrifice on the cross. See how the diagonal line which links the three crosses together represents the anti-Christ who denies the miracle of rebirth. Isn't it a perfect miracle?'

'It's crap,' I said rather dryly, hiding my disappointment as best I could. I can't deny that a little thorn of doubt had begun to pierce the bubble of my enthusiasm. I thought I'd start to back out. That's when I realised I couldn't move. A sudden fall of earth had closed me in from behind. I was trapped. 'How do we get out of here, Brother Stotig?' I said. 'Hi, Stotig, where are you?'

A little more earth fell, and I could feel it under the collar of my chasuble irritating my skin. I dug my nails into the earth but more fell onto my head. The light from the flash-lamp was about to give out. I was alone in the dark, silent hole. I now considered forgetting all about the idea of writing a biography of the Reverend Brother Stotig Isgis.

The Scratching at the Window

Before switching off the bedside lamp, Scilingo, a retired navy captain, decided to get out of bed to put a stop to the scratching at the window. The heating had been off for quite some time and so he put on his slippers and dressing gown before crossing the room. He peered through the glass in an effort to make out the little devils but could see nothing. There was nothing to be seen save the dark outside. This was the source of some surprise to Scilingo because he imagined the street lamps would still be burning at this time of night. But since he seldom rose this late he thought no more of it. Night made his window shine like a mirror, showing every detail of his face, and he proudly observed that not a hair was out of place. He hadn't seen himself in the mirror for a very long time. Since he had stopped shaving his locks, what was the point in keeping a mirror in his room? Tonight he saw a pair of eyes peering at him. He saw the deep shadows under his eyes. Since when had his forehead been scored by those deep furrows? A hand appeared, his right hand, raised to his face, stroking his unshavedness.

When he had closed the curtains, things returned to normal. It seemed the scratching noises had stopped. They were noises he could not tolerate, especially at this hour of night. The faintest whisper of sound was enough to keep him awake or to awaken him if he were asleep. He had not been sleeping well, even before the scratching started.

But now with this wretched scratching come to torment him constantly.... Who was behind it? Whoever it was would have to reckon with him once he caught them. He would have the full weight of the law behind him. They would see that Adolfo Scilingo was a man of consequence. He tried to think what time it might be so as to make a note on paper. As a rule, he could guess the time to within five minutes. But for some reason tonight he realised he did not have the faintest idea what time it was. He did not keep a clock, of course, because the incessant ticking would have driven him insane in no time at all. And in any case, hadn't he worked for the clock his entire career long? Wasn't it right for him to forget the tyranny of the clock's hands now that he had retired? He pressed the button on the side of his radio set, but perhaps because the batteries were spent all that he could hear was the hissing of the sea's waves. He adjusted the round knob but the sound was the same on all frequencies. And when he turned the television on, all he could find was fine snowy feathers on every channel. He picked up the telephone receiver to call the talking clock. He flew into a temper when the hissing of the sea's waves came down the line like the sound which comes

31

from the cavity of a seashell. Why could nothing work properly in this shoddy country? Hadn't he paid all his bills on time? What was their excuse for these shortcomings? He decided he would go out immediately and telephone from the public phone to complain. But when he tried to open his bedroom door the handle turned in circles like a bicycle pedal and the door refused to open.

He beat the wood with his hands until he realised that nobody could hear him. There we are, he thought, I'll wait until morning then and shout from the window and get help in that way. Such was his temper that he would have tried to climb from the window onto the tree's branches, but he had already seen to it that the tree be cut right back so as to keep its extremities from reaching the window. The birds must be to blame then. It was a disgrace that soundproof glass couldn't even keep the scratching of the birds out. The double glazing had served very well to dampen the dawn chorus. But not the scratching at the window. That's one thing it would never ever stop. One might think the window was wrapping paper, not thick glass. And it seems that things are so. After all, don't the birds nest in spring and turn very nasty indeed on all feathered intruders in their territory? Even on their own reflections in the glass. No doubt that's what all the noise at the window is. Small feathered bodies hurtling against the glass. A silly blue tit or a witless robin. Not worth worrying over. Scilingo had little respect for birds. And their antics were driving him wild. How dare they deprive him of his sleep each night! These things would be resolved once and for all in the morning when dawn had come.

He went back to bed. Eventually, pillows placed

comfortably beneath his head, he pushed the button on the bedside light to turn it off. Darkness washed over him and now his head was full of red and yellow sparks dancing before his eyes.

An almost imperceptible noise stole past the scratching at the window and entered his ear. It was a sound of sorts coming from inside his mouth, like the ticking of a clock. A rush of sound like bubbles in seething water. Nevertheless, his breathing was regular, like the breathing of prisoners in a deep sleep. Their breathing was always regular and smooth as they flew through the night air. The breathing of each of them followed a particular pattern. There were fifteen of them in his charge, seven men and eight women, all lying naked on the aircraft floor, all breathing nicely. The aircraft roars its way through the night. It purrs above the ocean as the voices speak in his helmet, giving him orders. The rear doors open: a nail-hard wind meets his face and white of moon his eye. Far below the waves embroider cross-stitches on the sea. He helps drag the sleeping naked one by one to the point of exit and one by one pushes them out. He doesn't watch them fall. Once his foot slipped and he came within an inch of following one of the sleeping into the abyss. Tonight he plummets again through layers of cloud and sees the waves wink at him under their brow of white and the moon like an eye above the sea. But before he wakes he slows and sinks easily down through chestnut leaves as raindrops pick-pock him on the head. He fills his lungs with smells of rain and watches the water leave snail-trails on the leaves. He is standing in the middle of a stony path between the fields and a wood. In the distance, a blanket of clouds shrouds the mountains.

33

Perhaps his destination is beyond the mountains? He asks the walker who is resting in the shadow of the hedgerow. The man does not answer. He does not raise his eyes to him or acknowledge him in any way. Answer me, he shouts, you must answer me. He remembers the shouting and screaming at night from the inquisition cellars. The walker is still ignoring him. What can Scilingo do but walk the path towards the looming hills? He reaches a castle, its doors wide and its towers many. Not a soul comes to greet him as he wanders through the foyers. From hall to hall he searches the castle finding each hall bare, each hearth fireless. Soon he comes to the summit of one of the towers. Beneath him he sees a rural patchwork of fields and wood. In the distance, dark storms near the mountain tops. As he looks down, he is suddenly overcome by vertigo and the tower stones seem unstable under his feet. He dries the sweat from his brow and staggers back towards the steps. Again he hurries from hall to hall looking for an escape route. When finally he reaches the ground floor he finds the doors under heavy locks. A key hangs in a box beside one of the doors and he reaches for it. Only with his fingertips does he succeed in touching the cold metal. Why does he always feel so cold? Now he remembers: he has been here before. And as he remembers, he realises that he has woken. It is pitch black in his room, and the scratching at the window has ceased.

He reaches for the bedside lamp and presses the button. Damn, the fuse has blown, or the bulb has had it. Does he have to be without light now on top of everything else?

His mood darkening, he has no choice but to pick his way from the bed and feel for the main light switch. His slippers are not where he left them at the foot of the bed. The rug is not where it should be on the floor under the bed. Instead of the rug, there is cold stone which numbs his feet. He reaches out to find the light switch but all his fingers meet are the rough stones of a castle wall. Very slowly, hand outstretched, he walks around the room expecting at any moment to come to a window or a door. But, finally, he abandons hope and finds himself reduced to lying down on the floor to get his breath back. And cold comes to consume him to the very marrow. In his misery, he asks why he must suffer like this. All he did at work was to follow instructions, like everyone does. He was not the one who devised the policies. He was not the one who injected the aircrew with a sedative. All he did was to follow the evening's rota. According to the rota that evening his work was to help with the pushing out. If he wanted to see his career advance, he knew he must participate. There could be no hope of promotion to the rank of captain without helping on the plane on Wednesday night. And he almost paid dearly for his services, did he not? He is flying once more now. Perhaps it's a different plane. He is sitting next to the window just behind the left wing. The sun is bright on the metal wing as the flaps on the wing's edge open and close.

Crossing the mountains, roads come into view below, winding their way through the gaps, the sun splashes occasionally on the windscreen of a motoring vehicle. Here and there in the valleys, the network of roads reaches some villages. On the mountain tops, snow shines bright in the sunlight, blue where in shadow. An occasional lungful of cloud passes over the mountain pastures. It's lunchtime on the plane, and a black gloved hand arrives to distribute sustenance. A plastic tray is placed on the shelf in front of him. A lid of foil is closed tight over the four-sided dish which contains the main course. This is the only hot food he has been given, best open this first, he decides. Carefully, he pulls upwards on the flaps of the foil cap so as not to spill any of the contents onto his lap. The forks and knives are a bit mean, but at least they are not plastic. He chooses a half-bottle of wine, wine of the country over which they are flying. He notices the fistfuls of cloud which are beginning to encroach on the window like sheep's wool caught on barbed wire. The aircraft has encountered some turbulence, the voice announces in a number of languages, and coffee will not be served until they have emerged on the other side. The mist swirls thick outside Scilingo's window and he imagines angels flying through it, their white robes loose, their feet bare. All the others are wrestling with their dinner. He looks out again only to see a face staring back at him from the mist. All self-control abandons him and he screams at the top of his voice.

Everyone turns to look at him in surprise. The scream lodges somewhere in his breast. What he sees turned towards him are not heads but skulls leering at him with large white teeth, black sockets staring at him instead of eyes.

Each time Scilingo woke from his disturbed sleep, he would try to erase the dream from his mind. He would hurry to wash and dress, and then step out into the street. From his table on the café pavement, he would see the mothers and grandmothers wearing black, and knew what their banners said, but he never approached them to tell what he knew about the *desaparicidos*. Perhaps he should explain, perhaps

36

then the irksome scratching would leave him in peace. He decided he would go to them in the morning, though morning was slow in coming tonight. In the meantime, he is stretched out on the floor, freezing in the dark, and the scratching has returned. The scratching comes closer with every passing moment. The scratching approaches him along the large stones. The scratching whispers the old questions in his ear like the salt waves questioning the rock and fifteen thousand and fifteen souls carry him like a coracle on a high tide and finally he comprehends that they are not questioning but accusing him. He knows he is not sleeping, and he knows too that neither shall he wake again. The scratching has reached his breast and the long claw is stripping his body of its night dress. Naked now, he is seized tightly ankle and wrist by the gloved claw and dragged over the stones. The scratching at the window has ceased, and Scilingo can already feel night take his blood's place and flow through his veins.

Rev and Hat

The mouth of the river is over a mile wide, and the small bushes on the opposite bank come and go through waves of heat and haze. All kinds of flotsam and jetsam wash ashore at the river-mouth: old furniture, boatframes, bodies. Were it not for the breeze brewing on the surface of the water, it would be too sultry to sit out on the veranda under the shade of the white canvas. Of course, the cool Pimms is a help, and it's nice to to be able to listen to the waves raking the dark sand.

'Excuse me,' said a little man at a nearby table dressed like an explorer of uninhabited lands. 'Did I hear you mention Buenos Aires?' He wore a white helmet on his head, a crop of white hair like a sheep's fleece peeping out from under it. 'A most interesting place,' he mused. 'Did you know that the name comes from the Breton *Buan hag Aes*? Well, the truth to tell, I named the place myself.' The stranger barely opened his mouth as he spoke, rather like a ventriloquist.

He rose to his feet and stood facing them. 'Forgive me, I haven't introduced myself.' He proffered a hand. 'Professor R.S. Singe M.A., Breton and bookworm by trade, and explorer of uninhabited countries during my leisure time.' He eyed the glasses of Pimms. 'On holiday, are we, if I may be so forward?' 'The Reverend John F. Thomas,' said John F. Thomas, pushing his glass to one side and getting to his feet to shake hands with the fellow. 'And this is Gloria Wilderbeest-Evans, my fiancée. Our "holidays" are approaching their end.' There was a hint of bitterness in his voice. When it had been established that the Professor was not a member of the old guard, more cool drinks were ordered, and the tall waiter came in his white gloves to replenish the glasses, bowing formally but with much dignity.

'You didn't much care for the country then?' enquired the Breton explorer. 'The food didn't agree with you, no doubt.'

'It wasn't that,' grumbled John F. Thomas. 'We were kidnapped. Dear me, kidnapped by two filthy, illiterate louts, and treated in a most outrageous manner by them. But they got their due in the end, the rabid old dogs!'

'It was a most upsetting experience,' added Miss Wilderbeest-Evans in her looking-down-her-nose voice. She was a big sailing ship of a woman, arms like branches, legs like two trees. 'What manner of horrible ruffians would ever kidnap a pilgrim?'

'Give up,' said the Breton, 'but something tells me I'm about to find out.'

And find out he did. It was explained to him how John F. Thomas had been enjoying his Welsh tea (a cuppa with a

Welshcake) in the Café Casa Marguerita hundreds of miles from the holy place where Miss Wilderbeest-Evans was traveling on pilgrimage to Upper San Marcos de la Compostella. And he came to know how the pair had become intimate during their internment, deciding ultimately to marry. Strange, the things that Fate holds in store.

Fate Higgins was a healthy pot-bellied man who had a sackful of laughter in a box in his breast. He had filled his jaws with gold teeth not by lying on the flat of his back on a bed of down, but by the sweat of his brow, and by his uncanny ability to recognise strangers who were good for a fleecing. He was a man who had been hardened by the relentless and hostile environment of the pampas, one of the 'children of the devil under the southern sun' to quote the epic *Salt is the Sea* by Bavar Bard. That day, when Miss Wilderbeest Evans came past Upper San Marcos de la Compostela in her van, Fate Higgins was busy tying his mule to the railings by the steps of the saloon.

But John F. Thomas was not in Upper San Marcos de la Compostela that day; he was seven hundred miles away having a cuppa at a table draped in red and white linen in the yard of Café Casa Marguerita in the shade of a large maple tree. His starch collar bit into his gills, and his wide-brimmed hat felt exceedingly hot on his head. He lifted the delicate china cup to his lips, and felt it tickle the extremities of his thick moustache. 'A goood cuppa,' he said as if his origins lay in deepest Montgomeryshire. (His was in fact a native of Anglesey, but had happened to discover an alternative dialect.) 'Dja wah me to do it now, Rev. honey?' asked Marguerita

Mimosa in an accent that lay somewhere between Gwaun-caegurwen and Santiago. 'Not yet, woman, for goodness sake,' barked John F. Thomas. 'I'm having a cuppa.' A jet of tea spurted from his mouth, settling in shimmering pearls on the nether reaches of his moustache. He pointed a thin, unwavering finger towards some dust that was rising lazily from the midst of the broad, featureless valley. 'There's someone coming, and he's no teetotaler.'

In the distance, a mule's long ears could be seen bobbing along through the dust, and occasionally a whip rose and fell, followed by the delayed crack of leather punishing the wind. 'Señor Morgan won't be here for another while see,' said Señora Mimosa. 'I'm sure we have time for one more.' 'Be quiet, woman,' he replied. He contemplated her before biting suitably into his Welshcake.

Meantime, Miss Wilderbeest-Evans has placed her arms on the counter, and leans over toward Jose Juan the relic-dealer, voicing her complaint for the seventh time. 'I shall not leave this place until I have been returned my money. The keepsake I bought is faulty. It's broken. Here's the receipt. Now pay up!' 'I'm very sorry,' replies the keepsake-seller, a thin, dark man whose withered expression seems to sink lower than his barren spirit. 'The money's gone, *desaperecidos*, you see?' He gestures with the back of his hand to the big empty drawer that lies open in front of him. 'Come, Señorita, read my lips: *no money left, nothing, never!*'

Strange, isn't it, how Fate can bring two paths to converge? Fate Higgins was busy tying his mule to the railings at the steps of the village saloon, and had just dried his chops with the back of his hand, when he saw a large, imposing woman with petticoats like leaves on a tree cartwheel out of Jose Juan's relic shop and fall in a heap in the middle of the street. He rushed towards her and offered a helping hand. The good lady struggled noisily to her feet and proceeded to beat the dust from her flowing skirts.

'Fate Higgins, at your service, Madame,' exclaimed the native, gold flashing troutlike as he smiled. He started to help her dust her clothes off. 'Take your mean hands off me,' she protested vehemently. 'I'm quite alright, thank you. Never have I experienced such godlessness. Each and every one of you is nothing short of uncivilised in these climes, and the Women's Institute shall be receiving a most unfavorable report on you on my return home.' 'Of course, of course,' apologised Fate Higgins thinking all the while, well what's a turkey good for but to pluck? 'Come with me, I know where you can rest a while.' And where Fate casts its shadow, Misfortune is never far away.

Misfortune Morgan cries *Hola!* as he crosses the Casa Marguerita courtyard towards them. Marguerita Mimosa is standing at the Rev.'s elbow pouring an arc of tea from her teapot into the eye of his cup. '*Bonas tardas, Señor Morgan,*' said the little dear, bending one knee to greet the tall and dusty new arrival. 'The Reverend John F. Thomas,' says John F. Thomas, getting to his feet and proffering a hand. '*Que?*' says the man, turning to Marguerita. 'He's over from the old country,' she explains. She bends the knee for him again and turns to go into the house, returning with an armful of tea

42

dishes, and sets the table nearest to John F. Thomas so Misfortune Morgan can have some tea as well. 'From Wales, are you?' he says, leaning across towards the neighbouring table. He stretches his hand out slowly, slowly. John F. Thomas notices a blue spider's web tattooed on his wrist, and a large spider netting its prey. They shake hands.

'Well,' says Misfortune, once he has draughted from his tea, 'what brings you to a place like this, Señor Thomas?' 'I won a holiday in Patagonia for watching S4C,' explains John F. Thomas with no hint of pretention in his voice. 'I came second in a competition to predict the future. The entire affair was filmed in Caernarfon.' 'Well,' says Misfortune, 'there's no use predicting the past I suppose.' A glimmer grows in his narrow eyes. 'Predicting the future, yeah? Here's a test for you: what's gonna happen tomorrow?' 'I only came second,' says John F. Thomas cautiously. 'I haven't yet mastered my art. About an hour hence is the most I can predict at the moment.' 'So you can't predict pain and sorrow for yourself in the next half hour?' 'Such a prediction I cannot make,' says John F. Thomas. 'Bloody hopeless,' says Misfortune Morgan, and deals him a loud slap on the ear causing him to screech louder than a pig whose throat is about to be cut. And in no time at all, Misfortune has tied him up with his rope and hoisted him like a sack onto the back of his cart.

The sun is already casting shadows over the café courtyard. The evening breeze whispers in the leaves of the chestnut tree. With a crack of the whip, Misfortune Morgan drives the creaking cart and its bewildered content back the way it came across the pampas. Before disappearing completely into the shadows of night, he raises his hat once to Marguerita Mimosa as she stands gazing towards him from the entrance to the yard.

'Miss Wilderbeest-Evans!' exclaimed John F. Thomas once the bandages had been removed from his mouth. 'Is it you?' He had never seen her in her bloomers before. 'No,' she replied, rather drily, 'whom were you expecting?' 'Have you been kidnapped?' 'How observant you are.' John F. Thomas thought he detected a note of irony in her voice, but he ignored it. 'Who would have expected to meet you here?' he said. Her bloomers were of the cactus-repelling type. 'Stop talking bloody nonsense man, and do something!' This was a command and no mistake, thought John F. Thomas; best to try and toe the line. Once his eyes had become accustomed to the dark, he could see she had been tied head down feet up to a crossbeam in the ceiling, the same beam he too had been tied to. They were both hanging by their feet from a cave ceiling like two bats. A wood fire smoked at the cave entrance, while the flames threw restless shadows. The smoke filled their nostrils and burned their eyes.

'I'll do my level best, but I'm not sure I'll be able,' said John F. Thomas apologetically. He started to sway towards her, trying to grip with his teeth the copious folds in her bloomers that had been revealed by the falling of her skirts around her head. He managed to build momentum in the sway until he had almost reached her, and with one more flick of the knees as he swung back, his pendular body sailed into her like a ball hitting a bag of sawdust. 'What's all this noise and shenanigans?' shouted Fate Higgins from his nest of blankets

44

by the fire. 'Knock it off! Go give them another poke or two, Misfortune, lest they forget that they're with *us* now.' 'Exactly,' said the other, getting to his feet, tired but uncomplaining. Misfortune was quite partial to poking visitors in the arse. He poked the two expertly with a long pitchfork. 'What have we done to merit this?' asked John F. Thomas once Miss Wilderbeest-Evans' shrieks had died down. 'That's what we want to know,' said Fate Higgins subtly, his golden teeth flashing in the fire's flame. 'Barbaric,' muttered Miss Wilderbeest-Evans. 'Want another poke, bubble?' 'For God's sake, show some mercy,' she implored in a, well, in an imploring manner. 'No,' said the two kidnappers curtly. 'Then what do you want with us?' she wept.

Misfortune turned to Fate and shrugged his shoulders. The latter motioned to the former, and whispered something in his ear, pointing to... to... 'Surely you don't mean to... to...,' said John F. Thomas hesitantly. 'To keep Miss Wilderbeest-Evans a prisoner here with you and have me leave and seek her ransom while you deprive her of her virginity?' A hint of hope sounded in his voice this time. 'Not a chance,' answered Fate Higgins. 'What are you suggesting?' insisted Miss Wilderbeest-Evans indignantly. 'Do I take it that you find the Reverend Thomas a more attractive prospect?' 'Be gentle with me,' said John F. Thomas, blowing a kiss. 'Look,' shouted Fate Higgins, jumping to his feet like a raging hornet, 'it's not your bodies we want, it's your money. What the hell do you think we are? All we bloody well want is your cash.'

'How much do you want?' Miss Wilderbeest-Evans' voice echoed from wall to wall like a bird in a cage. 'We only have

sterling remember, but you could change it in the bank.'
'I know,' said Fate Higgins, feeding complicated-looking
sums into his calculator. He looked closer at the screen. 'Ten
pounds and seventy seven pence...' 'What, each?' said John
F. Thomas, his voice faint. 'Are you sure that's right?' 'Well
ok then, we'll take that for both of you,' said the kidnapper
giving in. 'Fine!' agreed Miss Wilderbeest-Evans. 'The money's
in my purse. There's a twenty pound note and I want the
change!'

Miss Wilderbeest-Evans raised a white cotton handkerchief to
her brow and called for another jugful of Pimms. John F.
Thomas coughed into his fist and straightened his collar. It
was hellishly hot. He wondered whether it would be improper
of him to take off his jacket, and he decided perhaps it might
be. On the other hand, Professor R.S. Singe had been
permitted to remove his white helmet, and his great head of
white hair was standing on his head like a dandelion clock.
The Breton Professor shifted his gaze from one to the other
as he listened to the strange tale.

'A strange tale,' said the Breton Professor. 'And here is the
ring.' Miss Wilderbeest-Evans raised her hand to show it. 'Mr
Thomas wants to buy me a real one in Caernarfon once we
get home, don't you dear?' '*Buan hag Aez,*' said John F.
Thomas, proudly airing what little Breton he knew. '*Si, Señor,
Buenos Aires,*' said the waiter as he poured the drinks.
'There's your boat coming into the harbour now.' 'Well thank
goodness and *yec'hed mad,*' said Miss Wilderbeest-Evans.
Much clinking of glasses then followed, and they drank
deeply. 'And do you know the strangest thing of all?' she said

46

then. 'The witless, illiterate rogue had misread his calculating machine! The devil wanted ten thousand seven hundred and seventy seven pounds from us... but he wasn't used to English money, now was he, the stupid pea-brain. He was so thickheaded, they were both so utterly dopey, I prayed that John F. Thomas wouldn't succumb to his honesty and let the cat out of the bag.'

'Well, it was hard to believe,' said John F. Thomas, echoing her words. 'Do you know that Fate Higgins' mule was the cleverest of the three, either the mule or Misfortune Higgins' wooden cart. I've seen tadpoles with more intelligence. If the ruffians had only realised that we had access to every penny raised by the good folk of Arllechwedd towards the Welsh Patagonian chapels fund — more than ten thousand pounds cash in our keeping — I'd like to have seen their faces had they known that! And imagine the tragedy to the prosperity of the cause had we lost all to those thieving fascists. Thank heavens, it's safe every penny in Miss Wilderbeest-Evans' bag. A double occasion for celebration, don't you think? We have time for just another I think, before the boat leaves. Waiter, another jug of Pimms, if you please.' '*Si, señor,*' said the waiter who promptly took the jug and empty glasses and tossed them over the terrace into the river below. 'What's got into you, man?' snarled Miss Wilderbeest-Evans as she got to her feet. Professor R.S. Singe M.A. placed a hand on her arm to restrain her. 'Never mind about the glasses,' he said, smiling from ear to ear, his gold teeth flashing troutlike. 'Hahaha,' he said, removing the mane of white hair from his head as laughter bubbled from a box in his breast. 'Mis, mis, misfortune Morgan,' the pair screeched, jumping behind

47

the waiter. 'Call the police, waiter, call the army. He's a kidnapper, an evil man. Arrest him!'

The waiter remained calm. With much aplomb, he removed his white gloves, throwing them into the river. He placed a meaty hand on John F. Thomas' shoulder, the spider between wrist and knuckles all blue and sweaty after all that time in a white glove. He smiled an ugly smile. 'Where Fate casts its shadow, Misfortune is never far away,' he said, producing a long knife from his pocket, and testing its edge on his tongue. 'And, how are we?'

Miss Wilderbeest-Evans fainted. 'C'mere,' said Fate Higgins to the Reverend John F. Thomas, getting slowly to his feet at the table and motioning to him to come closer. 'I'm not very happy with the things you've just been saying.' He placed a paternal arm on the Rev's shoulder and leant forward to whisper in his ear: 'But I'm a reasonable man. What about we four all go for a little walk along the river bank to discuss who's a daft mule and who's a thick-headed bastard? Wake the hat, and tell her to bring her purse with her.'

The bushes on the opposite bank are still fluttering like ribbons in the heat, and the waves wash unhurriedly along behind the Buenos Aires boat as it turns from mooring to mid-river. Along the banks, the flotsam and jetsam of rubbish is oozing in the black sand, but nobody has come yet to pick through it; only tonight will they come, when the overbearing sun has sunk, and the suffocating heat has somewhat dissipated.

There Goes the Giant

In this story, the author plays on expressions from the middle Welsh text *Branwen ferch Ll?r*. One such is '*a fo ben bid bont*', a reference to the giant's lying across a river in Ireland as a bridge for his men to cross. A knowledge of the Welsh tale is perhaps requisite to grasp all the text's subtleties.

When making his confession, Bendigeidfran had never intended his accent to sound quite like it did, or his tone of voice to be exactly as it was. I suspect he hadn't intended to confess at all, and I think it no wonder at all that the chapel-going neighbourhood, fond of cabaret though they were, rose up against him, saw in him an enemy, and then buried him deep in the ferns, leaving him to count the stars for ever and ever. All this doubtless hit him square in the forehead like a coal-truck rolling downhill with no breaks, but 'bridge today, gone tomorrow' had long been the tune ground out by the ambitious hymn-writer who lived nearby. And anyway, ran the said individual's reasoning, what was the giant but a beardy old pagan, a wren-chick divinity despite his great size, an eclipsed god of the weary ancient world in need of a little pin in his big bubble. One thing is sure, old Bant, while alive, was rarely without his forehead, and rarely without his head for that matter.

He kept his head while all around asked when he intended to display it again. 'We shall see,' said the head from the box, and then sang like a bird sings of roving here and there, pausing to mention that he was expecting his father to call in. Well he knew that the essence of any good believer is the ability to stir the faithful to put all whose faith is weak to death. Pass through his gates and ransack his house. That was the kernel of his sermon in the box, but all he could think of was where's the door? The door which should remain unopened that is, the door beyond the waves where the river-mouth narrows westward, where mirth and revelry are to be found, and on special occasions, after a little ethnic cleansing, wild festivity. Old Bant had set his mind on improving his lot. But how? Surely that's the question.

Which does memory hold most poignant – life in a box, or a swing to the left? Old Bant looked at his wristwatch and thought, if he weren't living in the sticks, but were free to walk straighter paths by the light of day, he would be a good deal better off. He yanked his head impatiently from his box, and stared once more at his great enemy. Not all that similar to a wren-chick, he decided. This was a big man with a forest on his head, his voice higher than an alto's, his nose sharper than an Englishman's contempt.

'O man,' said Bendigeidfran as he saw old Bant's head

appear from the box, 'I know who thou art, and I shall not greet thee as a friend. Thy beauty is lessened, bareheaded and hairless. Thou art also a bullshitter of the first degree. A miserable, unmannered preacher art thou, and thy oppression is a burden unto this island.'

'Look here, you oversized pagan,' snarled old Bant through his teeth. Somewhere in the distance, a train sounded its horn. 'I know enough about you to write a thesis, and that's only your perverted sexual tendencies! Is it true what they... what they say about you and the ferret? Pity the ferret I say. Just describing your ugly mug would fill two volumes of *Critical Writings*, plus four more were the last word to be said. Just a cursory treatment of your hygienic shortcomings would require a sister volume for the *Who's Who of Wales*, with finer print of course. No dictionary could contain your filthy, uncouth language. And it is regrettable that you spoke of me as you did. And I couldn't give two hoots if you don't greet me as a friend. I have nether the patience nor the desire to argue with such an immortally stupid giant, and anyway that's my train. Goodbye.'

'Bye bye,' said the giant, waving at a pink candyfloss cloud. An old, grey hag sat enigmatically atop the cloud in gross contradiction of the europhobic union's new, green, rights-for-potatoes hygiene standards. 'A!' said Bendigeidfran, forgetting to be embarrassed by his height, because it's not often one sees a hag moving towards one on a cloud.

The hag raised a finger to her lip and whispered dourly, 'Do you have any more vowels, you giant?'

'Yes,' said the big man, 'a good many.'

'Then show me your relic from the old cauldron from a by-gone age and your dark pool and your two lake thingies, and your ridge near a wood.'

Bendigeidfran opened his trouser flap. As for the grey hag, she burst out laughing. She was used to working nights in the bars in Brest, and was a dab hand at singing melancholy seafaring songs. But she took pity on the giant when she saw him drying his tears on his apron. Maybe this really is one of the marvels of Wales, she thought. She handed him a document tracing chapters of his life that even he knew nothing of.

'I know who wrote this!' said the giant as he saw old Bant's train being sucked like spaghetti into the mouth of the black tunnel. He had scrunched the paper to a ball in his fist. He could see old Bant's head watching him from the window of the rearmost carriage. 'Go back and play in your lake, you stupid old fishing line,' shouted old Bant, shaking his fist menacingly at the giant. Bendigeidfran loosened his grip on the hag's cloud, and it floated up into the dizzy heights, and the hag hung on, and then everybody forgot about the hag.

'I don't *play* in my lake!' shouted Bendigeidfran, reaching out quick as light, grasping the back of the train between his fingers, and extracting it from the hole like a tape-worm from a ram's arse. 'But I do have fish,' he added when the two found themselves face to face once more. 'They live in my aquarium.' 'Of course,' said old Bant.

As it happens, the railway runs parallel to the lake's banks for quite some distance before burrowing into the mountain to reach the real world. The giant plunged two fingers into the waters of his lake and fished out two rather startled sharks. He put their heads in his mouths and closed his teeth on them. When he let them go, they danced a short lambada over the waves, singing soprano about losing some dog or

53

other named Shep. 'A couple of my small fry,' said the giant. 'Would you care to see some of my bigger fish now?' Silence lurked in the bushes, and cold dread in the rushes.

The silence was broken by the sound of a little alarm ringing on old Bant's watch. 'Hey,' he said, clapping his hands together purposefully two or three times, 'I kinda like your style. I'm looking for an act like yours for my cabaret. Are you free on Friday night?'

As it happened, it *was* Friday night. Old Bant was sitting on a high stool by the bar, while, behind the bar, the barmaid was pulling him a pint of real Stotberger lager from Holland. Old Bant was fond of Burgundy wine, and of clear Bordeaux red – he was owner of a small manor, Château Bant, one of those two-for-a-penny *petits châteaux*, where he was merciless unto the common folk, and father to many of his serfs, especially on Sunday, all going to show what a good Christian he was, but however fond of his wine and natives, he didn't want anyone here to know about it, and so, in the backroom of the Vat bar, he would drink only lager in case the locals might think he was getting above himself. 'I'll book you here and now,' he said. 'Here's your contract. You're on after the next act.'

The giant considered the offer. 'You're pulling my leg, aren't you?' he said. 'I can tell you're not serious. For one thing, I doubt your cabaret exists, and for another, I doubt *you* exist either.' On hearing this, the audience laughed enthusiastically, and one voice was heard above the rest shouting 'Interlude'.

'Thank you, Mr Bobyrt,' said old Bant, rather patronisingly. He stepped towards the edge of the stage and shaded his eyes with his hand from the floodlights. 'When you're as famous as I am, you learn to deal with minor frustrations, the small head of Mr Bobyrt, for example, feeding from behind, or with people who always want to steal your stockings.' He lifted the mike to his mouth. 'But now it's high time to ask the audience another jack-in-the-box question. And here it is. What do you need to clear great wide rolling plains? Yes, Mr Bobyrt?'

'Someone else's land, sir,' shouted Mr Bobyrt, keen as a kangaroo. 'Good boy, Mr Hobart,' said old Bant. You've won a holiday and a single ticket to distant Patagonia. And now it's a great personal relief to me, and a pleasure for you, here tonight to present to you for the first time ever on stage at the old Vat, and the task is all the easier tonight, as last night has been and tomorrow night yet to come, allow me to present, all the way from Harlech in Ardudwy, Benigeidfran Giant, feet grounded, to entertain you with his tricks great and small for about, what shall we say... half an hour? Give him a welcome.'

'Boooooo!' shouted Bobyrt, but his protest was drowned out by roars of approval and the clapping of hands, and hobnail boots kicking the creaky, dusty floorboards.

'Thank you,' said the giant stepping uncertainly from the left wing while blushing to his ears, the sweat oozing perceptibly from his armpits. 'I'm sorry about the roof.' He lifted the crowning roof carefully from his head and placed it in the playground nearby. He apologized for smashing the stage under his feet, then reached out with an arm into the sky and plucked out another little cloud to use as a pillow. Once comfortable, he continued to present a half hour of the most entertaining comedy and repartee that the audience at the Vat had ever heard or were ever to hear, and when it was

55

all over, the performer relaxing now in his changing room drawing deeply on a Cuban cigar, a gee-and-tee by the mirror at his side, there came a knock on the door.

'Who's there?' asked the giant. 'I wonder who's there?' he thought now, laid his cigar sideways on the ashtray, and tied the silk nightgown tighter.

'We are an unhappy faction,' said the leader, standing cement-like on the threshold, his followers ugly and behind him, some with their teeth sharp and protruding over their lips.

'Who exactly are you?' enquired the giant.

'We are they who should rightly have been the focal point of this tale instead of you.'

'You've worded that rather clumsily, have you not?' said the giant offhandedly. 'I have a right to be here because I'm bigger than you.'

'You're remarkably formless as far as we're concerned,' said the leader. 'There is no good description of you to be had, and we know nothing at all of your life and times. Where are the books that speak of you? We've seen none. Wasn't it a bit sly the way you snuck right into the story, and another thing, we think it's really dirty the way you were made so big.'

'To each his own opinion,' said the giant. 'To my mind, it's not that I'm big, it's *you* who are small. And you never answered my question. Who are you when you're at home?'

'We are they who were disenfranchised from the tale and we are now claiming it back. The following are we: I, Elfyn Oil, who hid in a bush when the stranger trod our paths and who wept on seeing his land fall silent, and here to assist me behold Tailor Red who stitched stitches better than any old cloth you have seen and who made a cloak of gold for the

king of all Britons and in his train comes Swaballt who needs
no introduction, does he? Oh and this she-monster here tends
to complain that everyone ignores her.'

Bendigeidfran considered these remarks without breathing
a word. He now opened his mouth to speak. 'I see,' he said.
'Well at least Blue grocer isn't with you.' 'Coo-ee,' said Blue
grocer. He was standing behind Swaballt, and this made him
invisible, because, as every teller of tales will know,
Swaballt's shadow makes everything that crosses it invisible.
'Oh, darn,' said the giant. 'I can feel things slipping away
from me here.'

'Yeah,' said Elfyn Oil, 'no more leader-be-our-bridge for
you – bye-bye giant sounds more like it! You're in the wrong
place, mate. And there's the door.'

The giant lifted his circus tent of a hanky to his nose and
blew. He dried Lake Tegid from his eyes and got to his feet.
On his way out he stumbled, trampling the old Vat completely
flat, and leaving the unhappy faction squashed like fishing
flies between two rocks.

'I sense I shall not be appearing on this stage much longer,'
said Bendigeidfran to himself. With that he felt his conscience
prick him. 'Don't,' he squirmed. 'Really now, I was a bit silly,
that's all, I'm not a bad giant.'

'I doubt that,' said old Bant, his head emerging from
behind the fence on which he had been pissing. 'And I'm not
paying you for your performance tonight for your information.
You can kiss goodbye to your one and six.'

'Childish so-and-so,' said the giant under his breath, a very
very big breath that swept old Bant to the top of a nearby
oak-tree, tall and convenient.

'Three hundred thousand microbes in your bed,' said old

Bant, sensitive as a toad in a frying pan. 'Twenty eight poisonous bats in your hair and seven pigeons up your arse!'

'No there aren't, you two-a-penny hymn-monger you,' said the giant in self-satisfied tones, having drawn a hand through his hair and inserted a searching finger into his odious orifice.

'Yes there are!' insisted old Bant, and he clicked his fingers.

'Waaaaaa!' screamed Bendigeidfran, dancing around like an oversized grasshopper.

'Listen,' said the respectable, overbearingly important theologian whose works have been closely studied without there having been revealed a single instance of swearing or impropriety until of late. 'Listen up, you lump, I'm going to count down from ten, and that's it then, ta ta. Finito. You'll be rubbed out, the chain pulled on you, farewell. Because you don't exist.' Old Bant looked at his watch. Bendigeidfran was still hopping around the place looking very sore but ever keeping an eye on old Bant. 'Ten, nine, eight, seven,' counted old Bant deliberately.

'I'm sorry, I'm sorry,' screeched the giant wildly, 'stop the count, take these awful things off me please; they're killing me, old Bant, they're killing me....'

'Boo-hoo, how sad,' said old Bant, and stopped the count on two. 'You should have thought of that before calling me a two-a-penny hymn-monger.'

'But you're meant to be from the South, Wil, you're no northerner,' exclaimed Bendigeidfran in his last breath but one.

'Hey, you're right and all!' said old Bant, and undid the magic for Bendigeidfran, driving the bats from his hair and the pigeons from his arse and the microbes from his bed and sending them all to Elwyn's place in Caernarfon.

'Fanks, Bant,' said the giant with his last breath. 'And for that I will confess that I do not really exist.'

'That wasn't the smartest thing to say,' said old Bant as he watched the giant fall apart at the joints and vanish bit by bit until there was nothing left of him save his haughty nose, forehead and head.

The poor ogre's head was buried not in Gwynfryn to keep the English from coming to the island, but face-up in a patch of moss near the border ditch and there it is until this day counting the stars.

'Like I said,' said the hymn-monger from Carmarthenshire from the new stage of the young Vat, 'He who would lead must be off.' As ever, he was enthusiastically applauded, and even Mr Bobyrt cried hurray.

Big Grey Water

The big grey water with its petty waves tickles the back of my neck and makes vexed tut-tutting sounds in my ear like a preacher's whisper. And I had also thought that water was a happy, colourful thing, not a dour and sorry one. I still remember how I delighted in it long ago. I remember how I used to love sitting on a sunny terrace watching the boats on the estuary as they painted white circles around the bay. I remember lying on the bank of the waterfall pools hearing nothing but the roar of the water. I wouldn't think of going to such a place these days. I wouldn't go anywhere near water. I would be quite happy never to see a drop of the wretched stuff ever again. But that's highly unlikely, because it's everywhere, just everywhere: nowhere can I turn without it filling my eyes to the very brim. I'm obliged to live immersed in it, amn't I?

Not that it's cold, it isn't, its temperature is fine, I think, because otherwise I would have frozen ages ago. But its uniformity makes it so tiresome. It's just so unchanging, so similar to itself, so utterly and boringly flat. Not an iota of humour, not an ounce of innovation, never a spark. Nothing but the same old dry, grey, featureless face day in day out. Yes, I know it's a contradiction, but this is dry water, and I say that having waded through it soggier than a fish for longer than I care to remember. I've tried the lot: patted it on the head, sung for it, told it funny stories – nothing seemed to work. Times are I tire of flattery and give it a good hiding, kicking and kicking until my shins are black and blue. Of course, this gets me nowhere either. The big grey water remains unchanged, saying nothing and doing less. And the barren waves lap around my ears and sting my nose and nostrils.

Things haven't always been like this, indeed not. I remember the time when the water was small. It would trickle innocently through my toes smiling mischievously in the sun. I thought then that we understood one another, the small water and I, perhaps even that we wanted to be friends. I would step over it, jump from side to side like a goat when thunder claps, coming and going as I pleased, playing to my heart's content and laughing together all the while. There's precious little of that now. Really, look how the bugger has turned out: one endless, ashen face, and waves, hundreds of measly little waves, all ashudder, like a man racked by arthritis.

I clearly recall the time when I could see far into the distance in every direction. In those days, the water reached only to my knees, and I was a sort of Bendigeidfran, treading on it, walking tall, the water struggling underfoot. Gosh, the wind would set my hair streaming, the many lands I saw would fill my eyes with colour, low ground and high, all in an arc around the water. Nothing would have been easier at the time than to step out of the water and walk over the land. Sometimes I would stretch out to touch it, it was so near. There's no point in my mulling over that now: better to shut it out of my mind, close the gap on all the many hapless, grey, repulsive thoughts, keep them out of sight battened down under the hatches.

But I can't. Before the water, there were so many nice countries everywhere, and friendly people living in them. The land south of me was low-lying. This was the first to disappear. When did it happen, I wonder? About the time the water had reached my midriff, that's when it was. I hadn't paid much attention to the lowlands before, because I preferred to look north to the mountains, or to the moors and wooded ravines to the east. I would afford the lowlands an occasional passing glance, and of course I regret this now, because my memory of them is vague, little more than a recollection of their having once existed. I simply happened to turn my head one day, and suddenly realised that they were no longer there. The water had lifted its horizon to touch the cusp of low cloud, and nothing remained now to keep them distinct, no line, nothing. I simply shrugged my shoulders and turned my gaze again to the highlands where, eyes peeled, I followed the path of the eagles I saw circling the summits as if suspended on pieces of string. And saw then the sheep, white and crystal-like on the moors, and, in the crofts, window panes glinting in the westering sun. I think it's the colours I miss most.

Yes, farms, moors and summits: all have disappeared

under the waves. One by one, as time ground slowly on, they vanished. Little did I think the water would claim them all, but there we are, at least their memory is intact, a memory of their proud, unyielding might in the beaming sun. I don't like thinking of how weakened they soon became, just ragged islets jutting out of the surface between water and cloud. I don't know when they disappeared. Until the water first washed over my shoulders, I hadn't realised they were no more. I remember the first wave which lapped against my Adam's apple while, for some reason, I raised my eyes towards the furthest boundaries of my world to see that, where once there had been islands, only water remained. Maybe I'm wrong, but I could swear that, about this time, the sun sank too.

For a time, I still remembered in which direction the islands had lain, and so I once decided to try to move towards them. But I must have been confused, because, no matter how hard I fought through the heavy water, all I could see was the grey tide on each hand, rising like a saucer mouth to mouth with the low-rimmed cloud above my head. The grey, watery waves and the skyshore had become one. My own feet and legs were one with the sand and with the large, invisible rocks. Grey is the only colour in the world of big water. If eyes could see me here, they would see me in a grey light, I know, and little wonder. And since, in a world of grey, there is neither day or night, one loses one's concept of passing time, and time itself loses its status and significance. I've learnt here the value of patience, and its price too.

The water is to blame, it rises so slowly that its changing levels can't be perceived. The only inkling that it's not motionless is the occasional intrepid wave which arrives some hours before the others which are destined to follow it. Today, a wave washed over my ear, and another, or perhaps the same one, splashed my eyes. The big grey water makes no exceptions: uniformity is its alpha and omega. I'll bet my life that even this wizened old water will crack a fleeting smile when the last hair on my head disappears beneath its rippling skin. It'll dry its hands and straighten its tie, and explain to itself in its own quiet way that I never really existed and that there was never anything here but water.

To tell the truth, I long for the day to dawn. I'm sick and tired of the monotonous water, of its voice growing in my ears and filling my head with lead. I've just had it up to here. And how can I tell, maybe I'll be better off below the waves. Who knows? Perhaps I'll see my hills and ravines once more, and eagles circling above my head. Maybe other summits will reveal themselves, coming like crystal flocks from the pen of night. Maybe, some still morning, when dawn is red and, one by one, the stars snuff out their candles, the sun will shine bright above me again. So come on, waves, lick the top of my head, suck my bone-marrow, swallow me up and let me slip free through your nets. Free of your preacher's whispering, free of the clutches of the big grey water.

Vatilan Dish Thief

Vatilan, the wise and unscrupulous dish thief, was the only one whom Nel ever really loved. Whenever there was talk of his prowess in emptying shops of their every item, Nel would stick up for him crying, 'Well, he didn't kill anyone, did he?' And when he killed Huws Parsley for the first time, her cry this time was, 'Well, I never did like the old stink-horn anyway.' No matter what Vatilan might do, Nel would stand by him through fire and water.

Vatilan was a cunning individual, as you may have suspected, and a very bad man. 'The end is nigh,' said Vatilan once to shopkeeper Gemp, a man once renowned for his collections of Quimper porcelain, though not after Vatilan had called. 'Uuuuuu,' said shopkeeper Gemp through the bandage on his mouth as he tried to force his tongue through his teeth. 'Talk some sense, will you, or shut it,' said Vatilan, before lifting a nasty knee between Gemp's legs and breaking a

Quimper vase over his head. I don't recall the shopkeeper's reaction, but hope the case in point demonstrates adequately the cunning of Vatilan Dish Thief.

'Vatilan,' said Nel one fine morning, standing on the tips of her toes by the great walls, 'I want to talk to you.' 'I'm not Vatilan,' said the ruddy policeman in his giant blue uniform who stepped forward from the gate of the copshop and stood before her. He carried a bucket in one hand, and a scrubbing brush in the other. He put the brush in the bucket, and put the bucket down. 'In no way am I Vatilan,' he repeated. He produced a booklet from his pocket and proceeded to read from it. 'Vatilan is a thief and I am a policeman called PC Ship.' He gave Nel a triumphant look and added in tones contemptuous, 'That's the difference between us both.' 'Shut your face, you daft cop,' said Nel. 'When are you going to let my boyfriend go? He's done nothing terribly wrong.' 'Really?' PC Ship feigned great surprise. He lifted the bucket and turned to the calamitous grafitti that had been painted along his cell walls. He started to scrub vigourously, the bright foam all adribble at the jaw of his brush. Suddenly, his hand slowed, and he turned to the woman who was watching his efforts. His look was one of uncertainty. 'Are you sure he did nothing terribly wrong?' he asked, wiping the dripping sweat from his brow with a big hanky. 'Certain,' she said.

He fetched his book from his pocket, and knitted his forehead as he thumbed and fingered it. Soon his frown unfroze, and a smile rippled over his lips. 'Right, well you're mistaken!' he exclaimed, planting a finger in the middle of the notebook. He wasn't much of a cop really, but he was fond of the minor rituals that were part of the job. 'It says here that I arrested him on several occasions for a number of crimes and that on no account should I set him free. And I quote: *we shall not allow bloodthirsty murderers to roam the streets unchecked.*' 'Yes, you shall,' said Nel, and kicked him in the shin. There's a lot of kicking in this story, so if you don't like kicking, do not read any further.

PC Ship was hopping up and down like a one-legged oyster and blowing with all his might into his silver whistle. Nel took the opportunity to admire the grafitti which the officer had been trying to erase. 'VATILAN INNOCENT' and 'FREEDOM FOR VATILAN' read the slogans in large red characters, plus another underneath them in blue paint that read 'PC SHIP IS A PRICK'. 'The truth hurts, doesn't it?' reproached Nel, and now she poked a fingertip into the middle of his stomach causing him to lose his balance completely and fall ignominiously onto the ground, blue helmet and notebook flying asunder into the middle of the road. 'Vatilan kills, not the truth,' cried PC Ship from the gutter where he landed. 'He's the one who kills, he's the one who steals and murders. And I'm the one who's caught him!' The officer was loath to admit his own failings; he found it easier to admit the failings of others and to arrest them as a result. That's how he nabbed Vatilan. Now he clawed for his notebook that lay open on the road a yard's distance from him, but Nel got there first and kicked it under a lorry that made a sorry mess of it. She kicked his helmet from his grasp too, and under the schoolbus it went.

'Now you school kid cop,' growled Nel standing one foot each side of PC Ship's head, his ears rubbed red by the leather of her highheel shoes, 'Vatilan didn't kill anyone, right?' 'Those undergarments you're wearing are illegal,' said PC

Ship. 'Take them off.' 'I will not, you vulture,' spat Nel, 'at least not until you admit that Vatilan didn't kill anyone.... There now, you can tell me....' PC Ship was having difficulties getting his breath back, and he couldn't get up because Nel's high heels had pinned his princely ears to the pavement. As he looked up at her long legs, he recalled a snatch of an old folk song he had once arrested someone for singing:

We're sure to pin his little ears to the boarding out the back
We're sure to pin his little ears to the boarding out the back.

The wind was filling her skirt, and were it not for the pain in his ears, he thought maybe he could have been happy there. But he quickly remembered that he had a job of work to do of course, and now he thought he'd play his best card and say in a cold voice: 'But he killed Huws Parsley, didn't he? I was at the funeral, I was in the cemetery....' 'Why don't we ask Huws Parsley about that?' said Nell gruffly. She stepped over the policeman and poked her head through the door of the greengrocer's on the corner of the square. 'Can you come out for a moment please, Huws Parsley, PC Ship would like a word with you.'

A man in a striped apron appeared from the shop drying his hands on a white rag. 'What does he want this time?' he grumbled. 'I have a customer in the shop. I'll lose him any minute and he's the first this week.' He stood hands on hips watching PC Ship who was sitting on the edge of the pavement tried to catch his breath. 'Well, what do you want this time, Ship? I've paid you your keep away money once this month already. Hurry up, I've got a shop to run.' The policeman raised his head and looked suspiciously at Huws

Parsley. 'Isn't it true that Vatilan murdered you?'

'Look here, PC Ship,' said Huws Parsley starting to get hot under the collar, 'I've been through all this in court. No, he didn't murder me, or kill me or any damn other thing, and these rumours you're spreading, saying I've been buried and how you put flowers on my grave every Sunday, well it's all a bloody nuisance and it's having a disastrous effect on my business. For God's sake, will you ever just give it up?'

'You're not paying me enough keep away money for me to give it up completely,' replied PC Ship. He motioned to the greengrocer to move along. 'Move on now, back you go to your shop, your customer has just walked out with an armful of your stock.' Huws Parsley swore and took to his heels after his former customer. PC Ship turned to Nel and tapped his nose knowingly. 'Well?' said Nel. 'Well what?' said PC Ship. 'Well are you prepared to believe now that Vatilan didn't kill Huws Parsley? You've heard it from the man himself, from the horse's mouth.' 'Huw Parsley's word proves nothing to anyone,' said PC Ship getting to his feet and straightening himself at the knee. 'Don't be such a dry biscuit,' said Nel sidling up to him and drying a speck of dust from his cheek with a silken finger. She wet the lollipop finger in her mouth and rubbed it on his cheek until the skin reddened. 'Come now, be a good policeman. Let Vatilan go, will you?' 'I can't.' PC Ship was starting to feel uncomfortable. He had lost his notebook, and unfortunately he hadn't learnt the reasons why by heart. He tried to concentrate. 'No, I can't,' he said again, 'because even if Huws Parsley is telling the truth and I have my doubts – even then I think there is another small matter left, isn't there? I suspect there may well be a further matter, don't you?' 'Really?' asked Nel innocently. 'I have no idea.'

PC Ship tensed his jaw muscles and scratched his temple furiously. It was difficult to think without his helmet. 'Another matter, a matter of importance....' It wouldn't come. It was gone.... He was at a loss without book or helmet, all bogged down, mapless in the middle of nowhere. How true the adage: 'great deeds stem from great needs....' Gemp? Yes, he's the one. Shopkeeper Gemp, of course, how could he have forgotten? Well, the case is safely in the bag now! PC Ship cleared his throat and expanded his chest to its full size. 'Shopkeeper Gemp' he said, and breathed out with great relief. 'O him.' Nel didn't appear to be unduly worried by this. 'That's nothing at all, don't you think?' she said offhandedly. 'He didn't kill him, did he?' 'No, but he did his best.'

'No he didn't,' said shopkeeper Gemp who happened to be crossing the road towards them at the time. 'He didn't try, you know. It would be unfair to him to say that. You know, my friends, I don't even blame him either – well, I was unused to dealing with thieves in those days, wasn't I, and I may have protested a little too loudly. He had to smash the Quimper vase over my head or someone would have heard me. And to give him his due, he did send me a card from jail to apologise for the vase. He wasn't obliged to, was he? For that matter, the vase sent me a card as an apology to my head. Or did my head apologise to Vatilan.... I'm not sure now....'

Shopkeeper Gemp started to rummage in his pockets. He produced an apple core and a piece of string from his trouser pocket and presented them as evidence. 'Very interesting, Gemp,' said the policeman. He cocked his spare pencil and made a note on the sleeve of his shirt. 'So Vatilan didn't want to kill you, isn't that right, Gemp?' said Nel skipping over to him and resting her arm on his bony shoulder. 'What do you

71

think of Vatilan being in jail for not trying to kill you?' 'Oh, it's a scandal,' said Gemp. 'You know what, friends? I've never felt better, man. That blow to the head with a postcard from Quimper was medicine for my doctor. He's been complaining of late, I've been telling him to try some of his own medicine. I often think that drinking my own waters is beneficial, you know – well I get it cheaper, don't I? And then there's the dishes. Well I prefer the empty space. No more dusting, no more worrying about them or around them. This new business importing ice from Russia is paying a hundredfold, so thanks very much anyway but I'll stick to that, health permitting. Crikey, PC Ship, are you on the lookout for a bit of Russian ice? The best ice, of course. You can sail your ship in it, ha ha ha... get it, Sergeant? I've never been happier and it's all thanks to Vatilan.' Gemp danced a nimble little dance up and down the pavement clicking his fingers as he went.

'Have you finished?' enquired PC Ship. 'Because I must take a number of these claims to task. If it's ice you're selling, how do you expect me to sail my ship in it? As if, as I believe you have suggested, you don't have real ice but instead ice that has melted – that is to say water, yes water, Gemp – then you are open to prosecution by the council's new department of trading standards. And to answer your last point but one, no, I don't 'get it', not at the moment anyway. And I'm not a Sergeant – not yet. And it doesn't make an ounce of difference to me whether you're happy or not.'

Nel applauded. 'How did you remember all those words without a book?' she asked sarcastically. 'Is that proof enough for you that Vatilan has done nothing out of the way? He's no thief, he's a kind soul who offers help for people to rid themselves of their material belongings and by doing so to find themselves a better life. He's also an efficient and expedient business man as you can tell from Gemp's new venture that was set up for him especially by my lovely boy.'

'The only thing is,' said Gemp, scratching his head, 'and I suppose I should ask Vatilan really, but he's in jail, isn't he, well the only thing is, and I'd like your opinion, do you think I should bottle the ice and call it water? GOOD WATER FROM RUSSIA. That's the name I had in mind. It's better than MONKS' WATER isn't it? You see a lot of the ice, well most of it really, reaches me in a not very frozen state, you know.... And then it's an awkward thing to pack in paper boxes and so on, it's all over the house, and the wife's left me after forty years because of it, and fond though I am of my water, as you will know perhaps, there's no way I can drink it all myself, you know, there's too much of it. And so I was thinking...' 'Shut it, Gemp,' said PC Ship. 'On your bike.'

Gemp climbed shakily onto his bike and pedaled off down the road in bewilderment. Nel's heart went out to him, but he had said he was happy and that was a good thing. Vatilan was the most important thing now, she thought; freedom for Vatilan. 'Freedom for Vatilan,' cried Nel, running at PC Ship and beating his barrelling breast with her small fists. 'Vatilan is innocent! Vatilan is innocent!' 'Now look here,' said PC Ship, grasping her wrists, 'are you the one who's been painting these slogans all over my cell walls then?' 'Come off it,' said Nel. 'I just happened to read them. Look, Ship, please will you give Vatilan one more little chance, you can have me as a hostage in his place.' 'What's a hostage?' 'All I'm asking of you is justice, Ship, that's all.' She started to tussle with him, trying to free her wrists from his hairy grasp. Her frock-strap

73

slid off one shoulder. Looking down over his nose, the policeman could see the shape of her back and breasts and her smooth dark skin.

'He was judged according to normal procedure,' he said dreamily. 'No, he wasn't,' she insisted managing at last to free one hand from his grip. 'All he got was you crying: *you are Vatilan and that means you're guilty. Jail for you.* Who gave you the right to judge people?' 'That's not what happened,' protested the PC. 'Yes it is, that's what happened,' shouted Vatilan through the cell bars. 'But it doesn't matter, I'm happy here.' 'No you're not,' said PC Ship crossly. 'Everything is fine then, isn't it?' she said, tossing her hair back and flashing the bluebottle a mischievous smile. 'If you're happy, Vatilan, we're happy too, are we not, you old spider?' She winked suggestively at PC Ship, and slowly drew her tongue over her lips. 'Yes,' said PC Ship.

She took the custodian of the piece by the paw and dragged him after her to the office porch. Into the waiting room they went, and sat on the long bench. Admiring the buttons on his uniform, she counted them one by one, then put them in her mouth, her tongue leaving a dull gleam on the bright metal. 'What bright buttons you have,' she said, thrusting her hand under the tight jacket and undoing the buttons each in turn. PC Ship had started to sweat again, and it seemed a noisy little aeroplane was circling his head, buzzing in his ear like a bumblebee stuck in a foxglove. He was feeling nice and drowsy. She had undressed him before he could say 'constable major' and he didn't seem to mind either. 'Which cell is the most comfortable, Shippy?' she asked making the keys ring like bells. 'Cell one,' he said with a frog in his throat as she led him away.

'You lie on the bed then,' said Nel, 'while I get undressed.' She started to unbutton her skirt. 'Well, are you going to stare at me like a dog while I undress, or are you going to close your eyes like a gentleman and turn to face the wall? You'll see all you want in a minute.' PC Ship obeyed, and Nel slipped out of the cell closing the door oh so quietly after her.

Vatilan came out of his cell and gave Nel a kiss. 'Good girl, I knew you had it in you.' He noticed PC Ship's clothes draped neatly over a chair in the office. Vatilan undressed and put on the policeman's clothes. They were too big, but with help from a safety pin or two, things soon fell into place. 'May I open my eyes now?' called PC Ship from cell one. 'You can if you like,' said Vatilan. 'But I wouldn't like to see what you are about to see.' He pressed his face against the window in the door. 'Horrible, Ship. Here, stuff yourself into these,' he said pushing his prison clothes through the little window in the door. 'I'll kill you for this!' belched PC Ship, endeavouring to hide his nakedness two-handedly. 'What will the Sergeant say?' 'Silence,' ordered Vatilan. He went back to the office and wrote an official report for the sergeant who was to call, according to his rota, that same afternoon.

When they had said their goodbyes to the cop, Vatilan and Nel went out into the street and made for the airport in the squad car. On the way, Vatilan, disguised now as PC Ship, was obliged to arrest the owner of a set of Llanelli dishes who was in unlawful possesion of a stammer, and he took the dishes into custody as bail. He gave the owner an official receipt and signed it PC Ship. Nel sold the dishes to an English stand merchant and with the money they bought a suit and tie and dandy clothes and two no-return Concorde tickets to New York claiming to be executives from one of the

Welsh quangos. They sent word to shopkeeper Gemp apologising for having made him happy and also for having hurt his head and enclosed with the letter lots of money to make up for the misdemeanour. They sent Huws Parsley a sizeable bank draft along with an order for a ton of bananas to be delivered to PC Ship's prison.

That afternoon, Sergeant Red called by Ship's cells to find that the policeman had taken the squad car out. Sergeant Red had been a fan of the group 'Kingfishers' in days gone by, and he enjoyed practicing his southern Welsh. To his mind, it seemed closer to the accent of the police in New York. 'Where *is* the goddam punk,' he said, searching through the papers on the desk. He found the note and went through to have a look at the prisoner. 'Thank God you've arrived,' said the prisoner dolefully. 'Hurry, open this door will you please.' 'Put a sock in it, Vatilan!' said Sergeant Red. 'Bloody northsiders! Listen up, I've read PC Ship's note here so don't think you can pull a fast one on me, buddy. He's gone and told me how you've put on weight just so as to make yourself look like him. You need your head screwed back on, buddy. Anyhow, WPC Wizen is gonna be here tomorrow — seems like PC Ship is gonna be outa the country for a while. Policewoman Wizen is gonna be taking his place — try and become her, seeing as you so clever! Maybe the banana diet PC Ship has arranged for you will be of help.' Sergeant Red left the office chortling to himself. Had it not been for the official uniform he was wearing, he might have whistled all the way down the street thinking how much safer a place the world was with Vatilan locked up in a cell and PC Ship far far away.

In April and May the Cuckoo Will Sing

I sat at the base of a big tree to watch the sun play in the leaves and to listen to the world. Peace is difficult to find, difficult to come by. I wonder whether the cuckoo found hers somewhere? Or is she still searching along the disused roads of Eifionydd or Meirionnydd? Or tasting the hot grapes that sink towards her through the cloud on the horizon? But anyway, peace has become a very rare thing these days. Be a shame to waste it, I thought, since there is nobody to be seen around the place, and no one wandering the beach below. Not a single one throwing sticks for their dogs to fetch. Yeah, I peered through the leaves and trees. The sun tried to wink at me under the cloud's lower cusp as I contemplated the acres of sand from under the branches. The sand is always so neat on a tidal beach, isn't it? No weeds growing on it, no castles sinking into it.

I didn't see her come through the trees on arched feet. I

didn't hear her leave either for that matter. Are you keeping well? she said. Difficult to know, I answered. I lifted a hand to shade my eyes from the blinding sunlight in the foliage. The walls are unchanged, I said, and the same old moss is growing over them. That's what you think, she said, yellow of primrose in her hair and blue of wild hyacinth in her eyes, but we haven't heard the cuckoo yet this year, have we? Maybe she'll come very soon, I said. Or maybe she's changed her tune. I suppose the countries she has to fly across are getting the better of her. I don't know anything about heat, she said, I prefer the rain. There's no getting away from the rain somehow, though it is nice to have the sun tickle your cheeks through the leaves as well. But what do I care of the weather? Foul or fair, winter, summer, I don't know anything of them. Do you sometimes hear another voice whisper in your ear?

She was eyeing me as if expecting an answer. What good does asking do? I said. Sometimes, she said, we do. Only when the voices are seething in the branches and filtering through the leaves. Did you see how I was searching for you as you stared out into the empty estuary? I saw nothing, I said, nothing except the world over there and then I closed my eyes for a moment and then I saw you here with me waiting for the tide at the approach of night. Yes, she said, but only leaves can open without being able to close. I opened my heart once, she said then, and though the hurt healed....

She stepped towards me and brought her face close to mine. I took his hand, she said, without expecting clay in the riverbed or the pointed stars. His hand was cold she said, but his forehead was burning with sweat. I dried it with the fold of my sleeve, but he got to his feet so that his shadow filled the room and his breath clouded the light that shone through the window panes. How long has it been since I woke? he said then. I didn't realise you'd been asleep, I said then from the doorway, because I knew by now I'd have to leave. I don't know now where he is or what he's doing. I suppose he only thinks about me once in a while. Sometimes I think of him too. I remember once, on the side of the hill, he came across the rise and sat beside me like never before... just that he seemed shy as he draped an arm over my shoulders, and tender as he kissed me just under the ear. Don't let's go up the hill today, he said, there some heavy weather on the way and the hill is bigger than I remembered. It's because of little things like that I can tell he does remember.

Nobody's life is all roses, is it? I said as I saw the colour drain from her complexion. She was staring out into the bay now, shadows shifting cloudlike over her eyes. She wasn't talking to me any more. Just staring into space, lips moving. I never offered him anything, she said, just my heart. I'm still trying to remember what my part of the bargain was to be. And I got my heart back in the end, a little worse for wear. The cut has healed over by now, and the scar is a very little one. It's small and white, just here under my breast.

And when she lifted her blouse there was the little white scar under her left breast. Love really knows how to hurt, I said, but we still always want it. Yeah, I know, she said, smoothing her blouse down. And you know how to state the obvious to everyone. Easier do that than say things that are vague, I replied. It's easier to love than to unlove, she said. O yes, I said, trying to think of such a thing. Easier cut the root than pull it, I said then. Thin white silk will soil, she said. And added: fault found where love lacks. Love and loathing, no mistaking, she continued. Can we stop quoting adages at one another all the time, I said. The ill when free of pain comfort lightly them whose health is failing, she said. Yeah, so they say, I said, doing my best to remember my proverbs. One swallow doesn't make the world go round, I said. One fiddle, one harp, I added. Enough is enough when the strings they are broken, enough is enough when the honey pot's open. Enough is a little more than you have, enough is enough to choke six dogs. And I shut my trap.

She was sitting at the base of the verdant tree inspecting me from head to toe. The sweetest song is each bird's own, she said and started to unbutton her blouse again. I didn't know any proverbs about things like that. Better two shirts than one, she said lushly slipping the thin white silk off her shoulders. And now her skin was shirtless! She whirled the garment above her head and flung it over the peeping gorse, and I looked at her there, bare-breasted and indignant, her eyes spitting lightning, her hands on her hips. She set her head to one side and the breeze caught her hair. So put it on then, she said, put it on over your own shirt. Come on, let me see you, little twoshirts. And she pointed to the gorse bush, and the thorns sticking up through the bright silk, just as the moon rose over the crest of the mountain.

I took the blouse lightly between thumb and finger, and its perfume was of May flowers, and I pulled it through my fingers, and wrapped it around me like the sail of a sunlit boat on Aber Henfelyn; the breeze was playing in the blooming gorse as the silk tumbled over me like waves of foam. Now my little one, I thought, she likes her blouses to be loose and trailing. But this is no mere blouse of a shirt, I thought, this is twenty Bendigeidfrans of a shirt, the great apron of the Anglesey giantess of a shirt, a parchute of a shirt, by gosh. You must be some sort of a goddess, I said, having found a way through for my head between two buttons, only a goddess could wear such a noble shirt as this.

The moonlight was filling her skin, and the sound of the tide was filling the strand. The next thing I knew she was taking off her skirt – I was still wrestling with the silk blouse. You get undressed too, she said. What? I asked. Why? Because there's a high tide and the moon is full, she said. Come on, we'll go for a swim. I don't like swimming in the sea, I said, and the ground is covered in gorse needles and it would be better to think of going home. And who said I would come with you? she said, kicking her skirt off, and picking her step carefully through the gorse needles towards the rocks on the shore. Come on, she said, the water isn't... very cold. By the time I had clambered down the rocks she had swum halfway to the island; I could see her, a white cork in the middle of the bay, as I tested the water with tentative toes. I'm coming, I said, trying to project my voice, but the breeze was against me. And the water *was* cold.

I didn't catch up with her, no; there was no hope of overtaking her as she swam like an incandescent eel. Maybe she's a mermaid, I thought, but then mermaids have no legs. She was waiting for me on the island rocks. Come on, she said, hurry. Where are we going? You'll see. Drops of seawater glistened pearl-like along her back, and her roped hair hung over one shoulder. I saw her white hand stretch back toward me, the fingers beckoning. We linked hands, cold hands. Some Englishman or other has bought the island, she said, and he has a great big house on the other side. And that's where we went – she knew how to get inside – and we wrapped ourselves in blankets, and lit a fire. Good whiskey this, well done summer-house Tommy, I said as we lay there feet entwined on a sheepskin by the fire with crystal glasses sparkling like stars in our grasp. We live in this way only here in these realms, she said. Which realm do you mean? I asked. The realms of no-man, she said. She pushed her hair back from her face. I didn't really understand, but I pretended I did. The realms of no-man, I said. The distant look of old had returned to her eyes. That's it, she said. Where there is acquaintance without meeting, and receiving without asking, and no seeking of things that cannot be had. She looked at me, and added, do you know me? Yes, I do, I said. You didn't before, she said. Will I still know you tomorrow? I said. There is no tomorrow in the realms of no-man, she said. Why not? I asked. Because there is neither yesterday nor tomorrow, nor watches nor grandfather clocks. How do they know what time it is then? I said. Quiet now, she said. We can live like this only in the realms of no-man. And you won't find it by looking you know. And mind don't you let it slip through your hands when your time comes, because that's the last you'll see of it. I see, I said, struggling to understand. Are you happy then? Yes, she said. But why, I said, if nothing is going to last. Everything lasts forever in the realms of no-man, she said. But you're the one that said it won't last, I said. The fire was dying in the grate and the window was grey with dawn. I stood up, casting a long shadow over the floor, and dried my breath on the windowpane to see the young light of morning. We could walk back on the beach, she said. The tide is probably out by now. Yes, it is, I said, my gaze lingering on the dark sand.

I wonder whether summer-house Tommy noticed the two

blankets were missing. He must have noticed the whiskey was gone. Our feet squelched in the sand and wild bedraggled clouds came up in the east. Hollow oil-like strips where the sea had been. Shore birds whistling. A piece of night lingering in the wood on the bank, and the songbirds' chorus drowning out the shriek of two lone seagulls out on the sands. My feet soft after walking on sand, and the gorse needles pricking me so that I hopped on one foot. She walked over the gorse needles without sidestepping and snatched her blouse from the bush. The morning light was creeping up on us from all sides. She put on her blouse and it fitted her well. I pulled on my trousers and closed the flap. I wiped my mouth with the flat of my hand to taste the salt. She stepped towards her skirt where it lay in a knot on the ground and shook it free of crawling things and leaves. The dew had completely drenched our clothes. She shivered as she pulled the skirt over her ankles and legs. I struggled to force my feet into shoes that had just gone two sizes too small for me. The crescendo of birdsong filled the wood and reverberated in my head. She combed her hair with her fingers and flattened it back. And raised a hand to catch a ray of the morning sun that penetrated the branches, catching it as if she held a mirror in her palm. She turned to me and smiled. I caught the scent of the wild hyacinth and could smell the beach. The light in the mirror of her hand was bright and pure and reflected in her primrose hair and in her blue eyes. Slowly she turned the palm of her hand towards me and the light sparkled over me and filled me with its bright warmth. I raised my hand to my face and saw how bright it was as if a flash lamp was trained on it. I stretched the other hand out to steady myself against the trunk of the oak tree. Its skin was rough and thick under my fingers. I could see the light burrowing into the recesses of the bark, wakening the insects, and sending them scampering to new hiding places in consternation. Much as they, I was unable to hold my gaze to the sun. The sun that smiled from behind a cloud at the onset of summer. I didn't see her leave. I thought she was still there and that I could turn to her and laugh together with her and talk of what we had seen. And I thought too that I would see her when the cloud lifted from the sun's face. But instead of that, the rain came tingling down, drumming on the leaves. Somewhere in the woods, pigeons could be heard mimicking the cuckoo's song. The cuckoo hasn't sung yet this year. No doubt she needed peace and quiet. I wonder whether she found it?

Translator

Diarmuid Johnson is author and co-author of books on numerous topics and in several languages: *Súil Saoir*, a collection of poems in Gaelic (CIC, 2004); *Defnyddio Agored*, a handbook in Welsh of OpenOffice software (University of Wales, 2006); a selection in French translation of poems by Dafydd ap Gwilym, *Un barde gallois du XIVième siècle* (Wodan, 1994); a Gaelic translation (CIC, 2005) of the Welsh novel *Sarah Arall* by Aled Islwyn; and *Byd y Gwyddel* (Gomer, 2008), a volume of memoirs about Irish society in the 1970s and '80s. Having worked at the University of Wales, Aberystwyth, for a number of years, Diarmuid Johnson is currently guest professor of modern Celtic languages in Poznan, Poland.

PARTHIAN

Award-winning
Welsh Writing

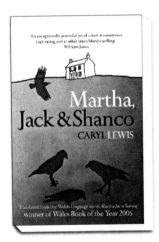

www.parthianbooks.co.uk

Printed in the United Kingdom by
Lightning Source UK Ltd., Milton Keynes
140497UK00001B/7/P